"I need to know you're sure about this. I can't have you regretting it in the morning. If you aren't, it stops here, and we go to sleep. I value our friendship too much."

No one had ever shown Marcy the sensitivity and attention Dylan bestowed. He understood her. Even Josh hadn't been able to make her feel this desire. The few men she'd made herself go out with since the end of her marriage hadn't come close to doing so. She wanted Dylan. Wanted this. Needed it.

She cupped Dylan's cheek. "I would never regret anything between us. You have my word we'll always remain friends. I need to live a little, feel alive, and I want to do that with you."

After closing the distance between them, he kissed her deeply. She wrapped her arm around his back as she slid her leg between his legs. It felt so good to have human contact. To have someone tell her she was beautiful, to make her feel desired. To believe she had something to offer.

Dear Reader,

Children's hospitals are by nature negative places, but so many positives can be found there—smiles, resiliency and the love of life. I hope you find all of those and more in this book. With doctors like Dylan and Marcy, a patient has every chance to live a long, happy life.

Having spent a lot of time in a children's hospital with my son, I've seen the amazing things that can happen. Through medicine, love and hope, the unthinkable can transpire, even finding the love of your life as my characters did.

I hope you enjoy this second book in the Atlanta Children's Hospital series.

I love to hear from my readers. You can reach me at www.susancarlisle.com.

Happy reading,

Susan

REUNITED WITH THE CHILDREN'S DOC

SUSAN CARLISLE

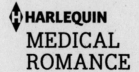

HARLEQUIN
MEDICAL
ROMANCE

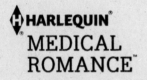

HARLEQUIN®
MEDICAL
ROMANCE™

Recycling programs
for this product may
not exist in your area.

ISBN-13: 978-1-335-73770-0

Reunited with the Children's Doc

Copyright © 2023 by Susan Carlisle

Harlequin Enterprises ULC
22 Adelaide St. West, 41st Floor
Toronto, Ontario M5H 4E3, Canada
www.Harlequin.com

Printed in U.S.A.

Susan Carlisle's love affair with books began when she made a bad grade in mathematics. Not allowed to watch TV until the grade had improved, she filled her time with books. Turning her love of reading into a love for writing romance, she pens hot medicals. She loves castles, traveling, afternoon tea, reading voraciously and hearing from her readers. Join her newsletter at susancarlisle.com.

Books by Susan Carlisle

Harlequin Medical Romance

Atlanta Children's Hospital
Mending the ER Doc's Heart

Miracles in the Making
The Neonatal Doc's Baby Surprise

First Response
Firefighter's Unexpected Fling

Pacific Paradise, Second Chance
The Single Dad's Holiday Wish
Reunited with Her Daredevil Doc
Taming the Hot-Shot Doc
From Florida Fling to Forever

Visit the Author Profile page
at Harlequin.com for more titles.

To Josie

The granddaughter of my heart.

CHAPTER ONE

"Mornin', Dr. Nelson," said the staff tech of the cancer center as Dylan pushed through the clinic doors.

"Good morning," he called over his shoulder, not slowing down.

"You have company today," the tech returned.

He hesitated a step. "Oh, yeah, I do." As lead pediatric oncologist at Atlanta Children's Hospital, he had patients waiting, along with a full schedule. And now a researcher was here to do a new drug trial. He entered the Infusion Room and pulled up short. Aliza, one of his sweetest and sickest patients, was talking to a slim woman with her back to him. His eyes narrowed and his lips tightened. Something about the woman sitting on a rolling stool looked familiar.

Dylan's heart squeezed when Aliza laughed

and smiled. Both were rare. For the stranger to draw them from Aliza shocked him. He continued to watch as the woman worked with the port in the child's chest and carried a conversation in the calmest of manners.

Who was this winning over his most difficult patient and undertaking the care that he or one of his nurses should provide? It had taken him months to get Aliza to trust him and this woman had already achieved it. What kind of miracle worker was she?

He approached.

Aliza's mother looked at him. "Hi, Dr. Nelson."

The woman turned and Dylan's footsteps faltered. *Marcy.*

The galloping of his heart had nothing to do with racing up the stairs. Dylan had never expected to see Marcy Wingard again, yet after all these years she'd turned up in his department. He'd thought of her many times during the fifteen years since he'd last seen her. Had compared more than one woman to her.

His startled gaze locked with her wide-eyed one. Yes, the same green eyes but with a wariness in them he'd not seen before. The shock he felt matched the look on her face.

"Dylan?" Circles of pink graced her cheeks. "Uh… Dr. Nelson?"

"Yes."

She glanced at the girl and mother. "I'm Dr. Montgomery. I was told you'd be coming in. I was just telling Aliza and her mother here about how I got lost on the way to the hospital this morning."

Montgomery? Oh, yeah. She must have married. "Sounds like I need to hear that story sometime." He forced his attention back to Aliza. "How are you doing this morning?"

"I'm fine." The girl looked at her hands.

Dylan crouched on his heels beside the girl's lounge chair, getting to her eye level. "So what's going on here?" He spoke to the child, noting the thin strands of hair where once there were beautiful yellow ringlets. His words were meant for Marcy. He was protective of his patients. Dylan didn't want other doctors interfering with them unless he was present. He needed to know what Marcy was really doing there.

He couldn't help but be particular about how his patients were treated or approached. Beau, his boarding school roommate, had developed cancer while they were in school. His friend's experience had influenced Dylan's style of care. He'd heard Beau's complaints about how he was treated and taken them to heart. Dylan vowed early in his career not to be the doctor who didn't take time to get to know his patients and listen to them. Even to this day he heard Beau's voice in his head when he first met a patient. Thankful Beau had survived to talk to Dylan regularly over the phone.

"We were just getting acquainted," Marcy said.

Dylan stood then spoke to Aliza and her mother, who sat beside her daughter. "If you'll excuse us, I'd like to speak to… Dr. Montgomery for a moment."

"Sure," Aliza's mother said.

He stepped to the nurses' desk and Marcy followed. He'd not seen her since college. They'd been lab partners their senior year of undergrad and he would've liked for them to have been more. To his deep disappointment, he'd been forced to accept nothing was going to happen between them.

"Uh… Marcy it's good to see you." He cleared his throat. "What a surprise."

"For me as well." Her words sounded more formal than necessary for old friends. At one time they had been friends. Good friends.

Marcy looked the same, just a few years older. She'd aged well. She was the one that had gotten away. He'd had his fair share of women since…he'd even been engaged and deep into wedding plans when his fiancée had broken it off. It still hurt.

"Hello, Dylan. I had no idea you were working here." She touched her hair as if checking to see if it was in place. The Marcy he'd known had worn it loose, wild and free unless she had to tie it back for their work in the lab.

He remembered all too well the brush of her long chestnut-colored hair against his cheek as they leaned over a notebook, working on an experiment. Today it was shorter. It was pulled tightly back and secured at the nape of her neck. He preferred it unbound.

More often than he wished to admit, Marcy had traveled through his mind when he least expected it. He'd checked social media a few times to see if he could find her, just to see what she was doing, but hadn't found anything but professional information.

"So you're the research doctor I was told to expect."

"Yes, that's me. Sorry I didn't mention that sooner. I was just surprised to see you."

"Me too."

"Dr. Nelson, would you please come check this port?" a nurse asked from nearby.

"Marcy, if you'd excuse me. I need to see about this." He turned, almost grateful for the chance to collect himself.

"May I come with you? I need to get to know your patients. After all I'll be working with them for the next few weeks."

"Sure. I'll introduce you." At least he couldn't fault her bedside manner with Aliza. If she was that good with all his patients, he could let his guard down. He shielded them where he could. They were already under stress and fearful, and not feeling well from medicine that should be helping them. Dylan pulled a stool near his patient's lounge chair and sat. "Hi, Lucy. How're you doing today?"

The girl smiled.

Dylan always enjoyed seeing that expression because too often his patients didn't feel like giving him a smile. "Nurse Racheal says I need to have a look at your port." He glanced toward Marcy. "Do you mind if my friend Dr. Montgomery has a look too?"

"It's okay," the girl said.

Marcy moved so she stood at his shoulder. "Lucy, will you pull your T-shirt out of the way for me? I promise this won't take long." Dylan helped the girl adjust her shirt so he could see the port clearly just below her left shoulder. He searched for redness around the site.

"I've never seen an implantable venous access port placed like that." Marcy's voice held a tone of disapproval.

Dylan ignored her. Now wasn't time to discuss that. Especially in front of a patient. "Lucy, I'm going to need to touch your skin around the port. You tell me if it hurts." He pressed his fingertips against the girl's skin, moving in a clockwise motion. Dylan made it almost all the way around before the girl winced.

"It hurts there." Lucy gave a squeak of an answer.

"I think we should take a closer look in the lab." He gave Lucy a reassuring smile. "Why don't I meet you in the port lab in a few minutes? I'll take this port out and in a few weeks we'll place another."

Mrs. Baker, Lucy's mother sagged. "You mean we'll have to wait to get this started?"

"Yes, I know it seems like a setback but it's only for a few weeks." Dylan continued, "Lucy's going to be fine. You wait right here, and

I'll send someone to get you when I'm ready."
He patted the girl on the shoulder.

He sensed Marcy's rigid posture as she followed him across the open room toward the port lab.

When they reached the lab and were out of hearing from everyone else, Marcy asked, "Why was the port put in that way?"

Dylan faced her. "Because I didn't do it. It was done across town at another hospital. Lucy became unhappy there and her mother brought her here. She didn't want to take the port out if we didn't have to. Lucy had already been through enough trauma. I agreed but warned them this might happen."

"So what're you thinking?"

"That it might be an infection brewing." His mouth tightened.

"I saw the small area of redness." Marcy still had sharp eyes. "Could be tunnel cellulitis in the superior vena cava?"

"Maybe but I don't think so. The situation is rare and that would be more so. We'll pull it out and try antibiotics then see. If you want to be in on the procedure you need to gown up."

Fifteen minutes later Marcy stood like a statue beside him. An uneasiness he couldn't describe circled her. Lucy and her mother sat in chairs against the wall, neither of them looking happy.

His attention returned to his patient. "I hate to say it, but I think you're gonna need to have a new port," he said to the girl then looked at her mother. Tears fell from Lucy's eyes. "I don't like it any better than you do but it'd be worse if we put medicine in and it didn't go where we need it to. Trust us. We'll take care of it."

The mother nodded. "We do trust you to know what's best."

Dylan smiled. "I hope we never abuse that trust."

"Lucy," Dylan said, "why don't you get up on the table here. I'll need you to lie down." To the mother he said, "Michelle, I'm going to have you kiss Lucy then wait for her outside in the waiting room. This will only take a few minutes."

The girl scrambled up on the exam table using the footstool. Michelle kissed and hugged her. "I'll call your dad and tell him to pick up some ice cream on the way home. I think we'll both deserve it."

"Chocolate syrup too?" Lucy asked, the fear still hanging in her voice.

Her mother gave her a weak smile. "Chocolate syrup too."

"I may need to get an invite to that." Dylan came to stand beside the bed.

"You're welcome anytime," Michelle said over her shoulder as she left the room.

Lucy lay on the table in the port lab with tears in her eyes. Marcy seemed to be having much the same reaction but was covering it better.

Two nurses entered wearing the same sterile cover-ups.

Dylan smiled down at Lucy. "Dr. Montgomery will be here with me today, okay?"

The girl nodded. "It's okay."

Marcy stepped to the table. "Would you like me to hold your hand? I know that always helps me." She offered her hand, and Lucy took it.

Marcy gave the child a reassuring smile. "If it hurts just squeeze my hand."

Lucy nodded.

Dylan liked the care Marcy gave the child. As if Marcy had been through this before. "This shouldn't take long but I'm going to make you a little sleepy first."

"Just like last time?"

"Just like last time." Dylan prepared the

pain medicine. He checked around the port after the nurses had removed the protective covering, and then glanced at Marcy. Her complete attention remained on the girl as if willing her not to have any pain.

He was impressed. Most research doctors spend so much time in the lab they forget how to have empathy for a patient. Apparently not Marcy. She was great with them. Marcy had been easy to be around in college. Her disposition served her well in these situations.

Lucy's eyes drooped.

Clipping the sutures holding the port in place, he asked, "Marcy, would you hold this open while I pull the port out?"

She nodded, letting go of Lucy's hand. Taking the long surgical tweezers, she held it steady. He gently pulled the nickel-size port out from under Lucy's skin along with the catheter. Quickly one of the nurses applied a bandage and pressure to the opening. Marcy placed the instrument in a dish the other nurse held. Moments later a nurse applied butterfly strips and a bandage to Lucy's chest.

"How long before she can have another port put in?" Marcy asked.

"At least three weeks"

She winced. "Can't you do it sooner? The wait will be horrible and her parents will be in a panic at the delay. How could this happen?"

"Take it easy, Marcy. We must have patience here. This doesn't happen often, but I want to give the antibiotics time to work. I'll place the next port below this one." He spoke to one of the nurses, "Would you tell her mother she can come sit with Lucy until she wakes. After that she can go. I'd like to see Lucy back on Thursday."

"I'll take care of it." The nurse left the room.

A noise from the area of the Infusion Room grew into rhythmic rapping. A voice sang out while the others harmonized. Marcy asked, "What's going on?"

Dylan stripped out of his protective covering and she followed his lead. They left the room to stand in the infusion area. A young dark-skinned teenage boy led a group of other patients around the same age all singing and taking a part. Their harmonizing sounded wonderful. They finished the song with a slap of their hands against the loungers they all lay on. The smiles were contagious. The staff and parents clapped.

"They're good," Marcy said.

Dylan grinned. "Yeah, until they make up one about you. Now I have to interrupt them to check on their chemo, then I have clinic this afternoon. You're welcome to join me. It would be a good chance for you to review charts and put faces to patients."

"I'd liked that. I'll review what charts I can and start determining canadines for the trial on Monday."

"Sounds like a plan."

Marcy moved on into the room behind Dylan. She couldn't have been more surprised to learn he was the head of the cancer clinic where she was doing her trial. She would never have thought in a million years they'd both become oncology doctors. Life had a way of taking you down roads you hadn't thought possible. She knew that better than most.

Dylan walked toward the patient who'd sat to the right of Lucy. He turned to Marcy. "Do you mind waiting here a moment? Dan is a particularly sensitive patient. This is stressful for him, and I don't want him upset. I'll check with him first, then introduce you."

Marcy nodded. She understood. Her son,

Toby, hadn't always welcomed new faces especially at his young age. Dylan's dark chocolate gaze regarded her before he gave her a slight nod.

Dan sat in the first tan cushioned lounge chair next to a window. An IV pole stood beside his bed and a small individual TV hung on the wall.

Dylan rolled up a stool beside the patient. "How're you doing today, Dan?"

"I am okay."

"Just okay?" Dylan pulled his stethoscope from around his neck.

He glanced back to where Marcy stood looking at the charting pad. Dylan tilted his head toward her. "That's Dr. Montgomery. She's going to be helping us here for a few weeks. She'd like to meet you. I think you'll like her. Would it be okay if she joined us?"

The ten-year-old boy studied Marcy for a moment then nodded his agreement. Would Dylan have turned her away if the boy had said no? She felt like he would have. He acted protective of his patients. She liked that. It showed he cared. Toby's doctor had the same boundaries. It was nice to know a doctor thought of his patients first and treated them as people.

Dylan waved her over with a small motion of his fingers. "Dan, I'd like you to meet Dr. Montgomery."

"Hello Dan." Marcy smiled as her chest tightened. Toby would've been about this boy's age if he'd lived. She couldn't help Toby, but she believed she had the answer to giving this child many more years of life.

"Hey," the boy said weakly.

"How're you doing?" Marcy pulled a stool up beside Dylan.

You can do this.

She hadn't expected to have so much interaction with the patients. She'd expected to do medical procedures, not to get to know them as individuals. Dylan knew them all by their first name. How did he handle it when he lost one?

Dylan studied the chemo IV line running through an infusion machine attached to the rolling pole stationed beside the boy's chair. "Dan, don't you usually play a video game?"

The boy quirked his mouth. "They forgot to bring it to me. It's okay. I get tired pretty easy, so I have a hard time not taking a nap."

Marcy blinked. Toby had slept more than normal trying to regain his strength after chemotherapy.

"I'll see that a nurse brings it to you just in case you feel like playing. Maybe we'll try to get a game in." Dylan patted Dan's shoulder. "You only have a few more weeks before this chemo round will be finished. Then you can get back to school."

The boy gave Dylan a sad look. "I hope my friends still remember who I am."

"I'm sure they will," Marcy offered before she thought about speaking.

A warm look flickered in Dylan's eyes before his attention returned to Dan. "Everything looks good. I'll see you next week."

"I'll be here. Mom says I have no choice."

Dylan chuckled. "Moms have a way of making us do what we don't want to."

"Bye, Dan. It was nice to meet you." With a tight chest Marcy joined Dylan as he moved to the next patient. She continued to follow him around the room, seeing all the patients there for the day. Each one climbed to the top of her emotional pile and sat, but she never let on. Instead, she focused on the children and Dylan's interactions with them. To her amazement he knew all their names.

The last patient in the line of chairs was a seventeen-year-old girl. The smile on her face when she saw Dylan said it all. She had a crush on her doctor.

"Hey, Mindy. How're you doing?" Dylan's smile was bright.

The girl's cheeks pinked, and she touched a turban on her head where her hair should have been. "Pretty good."

"That's always nice to hear. We doctors like to know we aren't making our patients too sick. This is Dr. Montgomery. She'll be helping me out for a few weeks. Do you mind if she has a look at you?"

Marcy gave the girl a reassuring smile.

Mindy's smile dimmed. She'd obviously rather have Dylan doing her exam. "Yeah, that's okay."

Marcy took the lead in checking the chemo setup, making sure the infusion level was correct per the chart. "Mindy, I'll need to get your vitals."

She pulled on her faded cloth hospital gown. "Okay. Don't you just love these gowns. So attractive. I'm going to design some cute ones when I get well. So that cancer patients can have something pretty to wear."

Pulling the stethoscope from around her neck, Marcy prepared to listen to Mindy's heart. She'd never thought about hospital wear for patients. They *were* rather drab and ugly. "That sounds like a fine idea."

"I've already started making sketches. Would you like to see them?"

"Sure, I would." Marcy moved on to taking Mindy's respirations and pulse.

Marcy glanced at the teen's mom. She knew the pain in the parent's eyes too well. That hit too close to home. Still, Marcy refused to let her pain show. She had a job to do here, one she planned to do well.

Years ago, she'd been like Mindy's mother. Walking around in constant fear. If she got as personally involved as Dylan, could she continue to hold it together? The next few weeks would tell. After all this time she'd believed that wouldn't be a problem. That she could compartmentalize the patients and the work, remaining unemotionally involved. Dylan's way of dealing with patients certainly wasn't that.

He'd finished up with Mindy's charting then double-checked her chemo flow. "You look good today. I'll see you next week. You don't have many more weeks of this."

"I hope so. This doesn't make for a great senior year."

Dylan smiled and patted her arm. "No, it doesn't but it's necessary."

She curled up her lips. "I don't have to like it."

Dylan chuckled. "No, you don't. With your attitude you should be fine. Be ready for the prom."

"Who's going to want to take me to the prom. I don't even have any hair."

Dylan gave her a reassuring smile. "By then you should have some."

"I hope so." Mindy didn't look encouraged.

"You just wait and see."

Marcy leaned in close as if to share a secret. "I'd believe him. I've known him a long time."

Mindy smiled.

Finished with seeing patients, Dylan asked, "How about getting some lunch with me? We can catch up."

She shook her head. "I wish I could, but I have some calls to make and a few details to review before I start this trial."

"Okay." She sensed his disappointment as his lips tightened. "Maybe later, then. I'll meet you here in an hour."

"I'll be here." She went to the small closet she had been given to serve as an office.

It had been nice to learn that Dylan worked at Atlanta Children's. Nervous and out of her element with doing actual work with patients—and more disturbing, children with cancer—she couldn't help but be pleased to see a friendly face.

Still as good-looking as she remembered, his shoulders were broader and sturdier than they had been in his youth. He seemed taller as well. What hadn't changed was his ready smile. It might be the one thing she'd missed most about him.

It had already taken great emotional fortitude for her to come here. If she hadn't taken this chance, then the drug she'd been working on for years might not see its way to helping children. She'd devoted her days, many nights and holidays to work. This drug must be successful. With it might come a promotion which would give her updated equipment, along with a chance to focus on cancer advancements in the future.

Later, as she walked down the hall, she saw Dylan standing beside the doors of the Infusion Room. She blinked. He was certainly tall, dark and handsome. Where had that thought come from? She'd not noticed a man in years. How could she? She'd rarely left the lab.

His head tilted a moment as if questioning her reaction before his look turned serious. "The clinic is located in the building across the road." They started walking. "I've not even had a chance to ask you how you've been. I can't get over you being here."

"I've been good." She wasn't about to tell him she'd lost a child to cancer or had a failed marriage. "And just as surprised to see you."

"You were great this morning with the kids. I was wondering how much experience you have with clinic work?"

She shrugged. "Not much really. You know how we lab people are—we don't come out much." Her in particular. Work had become her life. Her life saver. "Why?"

"I know this is going to sound controlling, but I still have to say it." Dylan took a deep breath. "Most of the patients we'll be seeing in a few minutes are scared. Their parents are as well. Adding another stranger in their life, asking them to do something they're even more insecure about, might tip them over emotionally."

"I understand." She didn't need to be told

that. She remembered her fear as a parent too well.

"Also try to speak at their level. Catheter is a *tube*. Superior vena cava is an *artery in the neck*. No fancy medical talk."

"I have no intentions of upsetting your patients, but I do need to have contact with them to complete my research. It's time sensitive. At some point I'll need to ask them questions. I don't have the time to ask you for permission before every interaction I have with a patient."

He stopped, giving her his full attention. "I understand that. I just want you to hedge on the side of caution."

"Then there's no problem." She held his look.

"What I'm saying is, this needs to be all gently and calmly presented." He started walking again.

She hurried to keep pace with him. "Cancer is a nasty disease that doesn't wait on us to be nice. We must eradicate it. What I learn from your patients can save others."

"I'm interested in saving *these* patients and doing it without creating more emotional scars. Like fearing life."

Emotional scars she could understand well.

Her scar tissue was thick. "I promise to follow your lead." She would until she couldn't. Her work was important too. The drug must be tested so that these children could have the chance to live when others hadn't. Others like Toby.

CHAPTER TWO

A FEW MINUTES later Marcy followed Dylan
down a hallway with small exam rooms on
each side. A nurse waited for them in front
of the first closed door.

Dylan took the tech pad from her and she
returned to the nurses' desk.

Marcy watched the woman in scrubs leave.
"The dress around here is more casual than
I expected."

"We do that on purpose. White coat syn-
drome is a real thing, you know. We never
wear them."

"I'll keep that in mind. I'm glad I didn't
bring mine. It's in the back of the closet at
home."

"Where is home?" Dylan glanced at her.

"Cincinnati."

"I like the park down by the river." He went
back to looking at the pad.

"I've heard it's nice." She'd never been. All her time was spent in the lab or at home sleeping.

He handed the tech pad to her. The patient Kristen Moore had been referred from a hospital a couple of hours away.

He moved into the exam room. The girl and her parents wore a terrified look.

Marcy had to admire Dylan for facing people almost daily who expect bad news. She'd been one of those people at one time. She couldn't do what Dylan did every day. It took a special person to show that compassion while giving bad news.

Dylan had always been that type of personality. He was supersmart and he'd made their long, difficult labs fun. She'd looked forward to going to the lab because of him. In an odd way he was one of the reasons she'd gone into research. He seemed to have retained his warm, easygoing nature but there was a hardness of maturity about him now. The only time she hadn't seen the humor back then was when he talked of his family.

Two months of labs passed before he mentioned either of his parents. She chattered about hers all the time. She was from a tight family. Even then she'd picked up on Dylan's loneliness where his family were concerned. He said he wouldn't be going home for the holidays because they lived too far away. They were missionaries in some South American country. She'd been tempted to invite him home with her but knew Josh wouldn't like that idea at all.

Marcy's lips thinned. She and Josh had been high school sweethearts, and their families were friends. When she and Josh got old enough, their mothers had planned their future: college for them both, then he would go to work while she went to med school. They would buy a house and have two children, a boy and a girl. She'd made promises to Josh even when there was a suggestion of interest in Dylan.

After all, she couldn't ruin everyone's plans just for a date. She didn't let it get out of hand with Dylan because Josh had been her future. More than once she asked herself "what if" where Dylan was concerned but she'd had Josh. She'd remained true to him.

Dylan's voice brought Marcy out of her reverie. "I'm Dr. Nelson. How're you feeling today? I see you live in Columbus. Are you a Georgia or Auburn fan?"

"Auburn of course. War Eagle!"

Dylan laughed. A deep masculine sound that warmed her, made her want to join him in his humor. "Well, I now know where you stand."

Marcy had no idea what they were talking about, but the girl's face lit up so that was all that mattered.

"Do you mind if I listen to your heart?" Dylan went through his routine of checking heart and respirations. Then with gentle fingertips he checked the glands in her neck. Marcy watched his face. She saw a slight tightening of his mouth. "This is Dr. Montgomery. May she have a look?"

The girl nodded agreement.

Marcy touched the girl's neck in the same area as Dylan. She felt what he must have. A lump behind her ear. Why couldn't she have done that with Toby?

Her gaze met Dylan's. He gave a slight nod then asked the girl, "How much ice cream can you eat?"

Marcy gave him an odd look. What did that have to do with the situation?

"A lot."

"Good. I'm glad to hear it. Tonight, here at the hospital, we're giving away all the ice cream you can eat. I need to have you stay here and help us eat it. Would that be all right?"

The girl looked at her parents. They watched Dylan with less enthusiasm. "Can I?"

Before the parents could answer Dylan said gently, "Kristen will need to come in for some tests."

A stricken look showed on their faces as their worst fear became reality. Marcy's heart went out to them.

"Someone'll come in to show you where to go." Dylan made some notes on the pad then smiled at the girl. "I'll want to know tomorrow how much of that ice cream you ate."

A few minutes later Marcy followed him out of the room. "That was well done, Dr. Nelson. You had her thinking about ice cream instead of being poked and prodded."

"I'd say thank you, but I hate the thought of the road the girl has ahead of her."

"Then why did you go into oncology?"

"Because I had a friend in boarding school who had cancer. I remember how scared he was. He told me what it was like. How he hated the way doctors treated him like an experiment all the time. That he wanted them to see him as a person. Talk to him so he could understand, not speak over his head.

And most of all tell him the truth. When I started this work, I promised myself I'd remember his words."

"How's he doing now?"

"Great. He has a wife and family. Still, having cancer changed his life."

"Cancer will do that." She knew too well.

Dylan gave her a questioning look. Had he heard in that statement more than she wanted to share? He started toward the next exam room. "Why did you decide to go into cancer research?"

"For the same reason as you. To help children." What she didn't say was that these days it was to redeem herself for the past, to keep the guilt at bay. "And for their parents. They suffer too."

"They do. Sometimes more than the patients." The pain he'd seen was evident in his voice.

They spent the rest of the afternoon seeing patients. Many had to have lab work and return in three to six months. Some were patients who recovered from cancer and were returning for checkups. Marcy couldn't deny she was wrung out afterward. She still needed to get to her tiny office and start working on which patients would qualify for the trial, which included checking her emails and a call to her lab.

"Do you have plans this weekend? I feel as if I should welcome you to Atlanta. Take you to dinner or something. After all, we're old friends," Dylan said as they were walking back to the hospital.

"I wish I could, but I have a lot of work to do. Especially after meeting patients today."

"Okay, but you know the old saying all work and no play or meals makes for a dull doctor."

Marcy couldn't help but smile. "I'm not sure that's how it goes but I get your meaning. But I still have work to do."

A few minutes later she entered and closed the office door behind her. She looked at her shaking hands. Taking in a couple of deep breaths, she brought her nerves under control. With each new patient it had become more difficult for her to keep her emotions behind a curtain. Dylan would have been confused if she'd broken down in tears. She had no idea venturing outside of the lab would be so difficult emotionally, yet as the afternoon progressed her nerves eased and her confidence increased. Here she understood the parents and patients.

If she wanted this research to be successful, she had to see it through. This was not
only her chance for promotion, but she believed TM13 would help children live. She
would be in town for six weeks but believed
with three months of good solid numbers she
could get the Food and Drug Administration's
approval.

Monday morning, Dylan took the back way
to his office in the cancer center. Over the
weekend he'd pondered the return of Marcy
to his life as he did chores, worked on his
car and watched a couple of football games.
She'd broken his heart years before, but she'd
never known it.

He'd learned early in life to cover his emotions. Few knew how much he missed his
family while he was in boarding school, or
how much he suffered over Beau having cancer. By the time he met Marcy he'd mastered
not letting anyone know his true feelings. Not
that she would have been interested since
she'd had a boyfriend. For all he knew now
she had a husband and children waiting for
her to come home.

None of that was his business anyway.
They were colleagues, that was all. Yet he

couldn't help being curious about her life since they'd last seen each other. Couldn't help finding her attractive still.

He was in his office catching up on a few emails and reviewing his patient list when a knock at his door drew his attention.

"Hey," Marcy said.

Today she wore a simple blouse, pants that hugged her slim hips and flat shoes, not her power suit of the other day. He liked this more relaxed version better. She looked approachable and fragile, but she was thin, too thin really.

She continued to stand in the doorway. "Sorry to bother you."

"No bother. You're here early. How can I help?"

"I just have a few questions about some of your patients."

He waved a hand toward the lone chair in front of his desk. "What do you want to know?"

She took a seat and swiped open her tech pad. "Tell me about Roger Harris. He seems like a good candidate."

"Yes, I believe he would be. He's just starting chemo."

She made a note on her pad. "What about Rena McCray?"

"I don't think so." Dylan clasped his hands and rested his chin on his fingertips. "This is her second round. She isn't reacting well to the treatment."

"Then she might just benefit from TM13."

He gave that thought. "I'll review her latest labs and let you know."

"Robert Neels."

"Robby." He corrected. "He's the guy who led the rap."

"Oh, I know who he is now." She looked up at Dylan. "Robby. He seems on the cusp of recovery, but his labs weren't good last time."

"No, they weren't. How many of these do you have?"

"I managed to get through twenty-three this morning." Marcy looked at her pad again.

Dylan pushed back from his desk. "Have you been here all weekend working?"

"Most of it. I wanted to get started on this trial."

His eyes narrowed in concern. "Is there some urgency that requires you to work all weekend and be here so early?"

"Just patients like that beautiful girl going through chemo. It amazes me she could still talk about designing clothes as sick as she's been. That she still has dreams while having chemo and losing all her hair. I think TM13 can help her."

"I already have a very high success rate." Dylan couldn't help but defend his program.

"I'm aware of your success. But I'm also aware of the struggle."

He nodded solemnly, conscious of something in her tone he couldn't quite identify. "That's true. You're just not used to working with the patients. It's easy to think of cancer in the abstract when you're in a lab poking around with test tubes but it gets personal when you deal with patients. Especially when they're children."

"I understand you have clinic again this afternoon."

"I do."

Her eyelids flicked up. "I'll be there. I'll be ready to start the new medicine trial as soon as we have all the agreements."

Dylan leaned back in his chair. "We can discuss it with the parents as we work through patients today."

Marcy turned off the pad. "Great. I'll review all their charts tonight."

Dylan's brows came together but he said

nothing. He believed in working hard but she was taking it to an entirely different level.

She looked at him. "Should I meet you at the clinic?"

"Why don't I come get you? We need to go to a different area today. What hole did they stick you in and called it an office?"

Marcy looked around his space. "The room off the conference room."

His eyes went wide with disbelief. "You mean the closet? Surely there's some place better than that."

"I'm making it work. It's better than nothing. It's nothing like your palatial office."

He huffed and then grinned. His office was functional at best, but it was large. "Finally, the Marcy I remember. Able to put me in my place." Oddly he liked that familiar teasing part of Marcy. Too much.

But why didn't that humor reach her eyes? The sparkle and delight she'd once had for life had dimmed. He'd viewed those emotions clearly on their graduation day. He only attended the ceremony so he could see her one last time. He had no family attending so he thought to share part of the day with her.

He'd found Marcy in the crowd of students wearing black robes and hurried in her direction. Just before he reached her, Marcy broke away from the group and ran into the arms of a man who had walked up. It had to be the boyfriend she'd told him about when he'd dared to ask her out. Dylan didn't bother to speak, and instead he melted into the crowd.

It wasn't her fault he'd hurt so much that day, but one thing was for sure, he wouldn't let her do that to him again.

Two days later, at a quick knock on her door, Marcy looked up to see Dylan. He stuck his head inside the supply closet turned office. "It's lunchtime. Want to…" The pleasant look left his face and was replaced with a comic look of horror. "This place is awful. How do you get any work done?"

"It's not so bad."

"You have a broad idea of bad."

Marcy chuckled. "What were you saying about something to eat?"

"I wanted to see if you would like to join me in the cafeteria."

She had to admit she was hungry. And curious about Dylan's life since college too. Was he married? She hadn't heard him say anything about a family. She'd always thought he was the type who would want a family.

Dylan surveyed the space with shelves on both sides. "You need more room than this."

"This was all that was available."

He huffed. "I have an idea. I don't use my office much. You're welcome to share mine. At least you wouldn't have to worry about people disturbing you to get to office supplies."

"I can't take your office." Marcy's denial was quick.

"You won't be. Anyway, you'll only be here for a little while. I insist."

Sharing an office with Dylan didn't sound like a good idea but at least she wouldn't be constantly disturbed. "I guess so. Since you insist."

Dylan shrugged. "Okay. We'll get it done first chance we get. You ready for some food?"

She gave him a weak smile. "If I remember correctly, you thought of little more than food when we were in college."

He sobered. "I thought of other things. But I do like a good meal." A grin popped out again.

She watched Dylan settle into an orange plastic utilitarian chair across the metal table from her in the cafeteria. Other staff dressed in surgical scrubs and office wear came and went around them.

"I can't believe that after all these years you show up in my hospital. And of all places my department. What have you been doing all this time?" Dylan sounded interested, instead of interrogative.

"Same as you, I'm sure. Medical school, fellowship and I got a job." She forked a piece of lettuce.

"Where did you go to medical school?" He took a bite out of his sandwich.

"Duke."

Dylan brows rose. "Impressive. They're doing great work there."

"They are." Marcy relaxed and took a forkful of her salad.

"Did you like living in North Carolina?"

It had been the perfect place for Josh to get a job with all the high-tech business in the area while she went to medical school. It was even a great place to raise a family. She never planned to return. After she finished chewing, she said, "I did. Enough about me. How about you? Where did you get your medical training?"

"NYU."

"That's impressive too." She smiled. He'd

been smart enough in college to get into any medical school he wished. "Who would have thought that two kids in a lab class in a small midwestern college would have both become doctors and work in the cancer field?"

"It's a small world." He continued to eat his sandwich. "What made you go into research?"

"I just always liked lab work. Cancer needs to be eradicated." The words were as flat and dry as a Texas dirt road in the summer. She didn't dare let the emotion she felt show, or she might fall apart.

"Always liked? I must be remembering wrong. You dreaded labs in college."

"Let's just say I learned to appreciate them." Because of him. She looked forward to going to lab because she had a chance to see Dylan. Almost engaged to Josh, she shouldn't have had those thoughts, but she had.

"I always saw you as someone who liked to be around people. I thought you would have gravitated toward patients." He watched her closely.

"I'm not as good with them as you are. You always had a way of making people feel valued even back then."

Dylan grinned. "You made lab my favorite class. We had a good time."

She smiled. It had been too long since she thought of those carefree days. The days before...

"Yes, we did."

He nodded. "After med school you joined the private lab company CanMed? Or was there a stop in between?"

Marcy pushed her salad away half-finished. "CanMed hired me straight out of medical school." She'd begged for the job. The desire to help find the cure to cancer burned in her, drove her.

He leaned back in his chair. "And that's what brings you to my door."

"Yes. Your hospital agreed to be a part of the TM13 trial."

He took a sip of his drink. "Which I understand is a new regime with fewer side effects and better outcomes."

Her gaze rose to meet his. She couldn't help the pride in her voice as she said, "Yes. My team developed it."

"Impressive." Dylan grinned.

"We've had outstanding success in the lab. I'm hoping for the same or better results in actual use."

He swallowed the bite. "I hope that's what we see also."

"I'm sure you do. I've seen how important your patients are to you." She met his eyes, noticing again the warmth in the dark chocolate depths.

"I'm sorry if I've been rough on you. I'd like to say I'll mellow some, but you'd be safer with just learning to deal with me. I'm protective and don't apologize for it."

She pursed her lips and nodded. "That's a positive attribute, but I'll admit it takes some getting used to."

He laughed. Loud enough to attract the attention of those around them. "Now, there's another part of the Marcy I remember. She didn't mind saying what she thought. Enough about work. Tell me, did you end up marrying that guy you were dating in college?"

The abrupt change in topic took her by surprise for a moment. "Yes, we were married for five years. And divorced years ago."

"I'm sorry to hear that." He sounded sincere.

Her lips thinned. "Those things happen."

His look met hers. "You were devoted to him when we were in college."

Her gaze dropped to her food tray. "Yeah, but life happens."

Dylan gave her a long studying look that made her squirm. She closed the preprepared salad plastic container and stared back at him. "How about you, Dr. Nelson. Is there a wife or someone special in your life?"

"Nope. I've had a couple of close calls but never made it down the aisle."

"I'm sorry to hear that, I'm sure they were too."

He chuckled. "I think it was more like they got away clean."

"That couldn't be true." It was hard to believe he hadn't been snatched up.

"Let's just say they wanted to be married to a doctor more for social reasons than because they cared about me. They expected me to be more into social engagements than my work."

"You never said anything about being interested in working with children when we were in college. But now I think about it I'm not surprised." She crossed her arms on the table, examining him as if seeing him for the first time. His easy charm and cheeky sense of humor were clear assets in the field he'd chosen to specialize in.

"Are you saying I acted like a child?" He grinned.

Marcy shook her head. "You're not going to pull me into that discussion. How did you end up here?"

"After I finished med school, I did my fellowship here and stayed."

"So you're an important part of what makes the cancer program here so good?"

He shrugged. "I guess so. But it's really the children and their parents who are the stars."

Marcy didn't feel like a star. She felt like a failure. Maybe when TM13 showed what she believed it would, that would change. That was her single focus. "We better get back to work. I have a meeting to prepare for."

CHAPTER THREE

THE NEXT DAY Dylan entered the clinic exam room followed by Marcy. "Hi, Lucy. How're you feeling?"

The girl looked at her mother then said so low he almost couldn't hear her, "Fine."

"That's good to hear. I forgot to ask the other day, do you have a dog?"

"Yes."

"You do?" Dylan's voice rose an octave.

The girl nodded.

"Is he brown or black? I've been thinking about getting a black dog but I'm not sure that's the right color."

"Mine is brown and white. His name is Rusty."

Dylan smiled. "I like that name. Does he have a rusty color?"

Lucy nodded.

"Maybe if I get a black dog, I'll name him Blackie. What do you think about that?"

Lucy brightened. "Blackie would be a good name."

He glanced a Marcy. She wore a slight smile on her lips.

"I think so too." Dylan turned serious. "Now that you've helped me with a new dog, may I have a look at where I took out the port?"

"Okay."

"Do you mind sitting on the exam table?" Dylan placed his hand on the cushioned table.

Lucy shook her head and climbed up to sit with her legs swinging over the side.

"Now I'd like you to pull your shirt up so that I can see where the port was."

The girl did as he asked. As he stepped closer, Marcy moved beside him. "The site looks good. Healing well. The antibiotics are working." He shifted.

Marcy took the spot. "May I touch, Lucy?" She nodded.

Marcy pulled a plastic glove out of the box on the wall then pulled it on. "You tell me if I hurt you." Marcy pushed around the area.

Lucy had no reaction.

Marcy stepped back, giving him a look of satisfaction.

Dylan couldn't help but be pleased and he'd really done nothing. "Mrs. Baker, Dr. Montgomery and I would like to discuss a new drug that we'd like to try on Lucy when she starts her treatment at the end of next week."

The mother sat straighter. "I thought it would be another two weeks?"

"I believed so too, but Lucy's port area is looking well enough that I think we can do it a few days earlier," Dylan explained, gesturing to Marcy.

She sat on a chair beside Mrs. Baker. "I'm a research doctor, and I've developed a new drug. I believe that it can help Lucy. I'd like to enroll her in my trial. We've had great success in the lab and I think Lucy can benefit from the drug."

Mrs. Baker looked unconvinced. "I don't know… Lucy has already had a port in. Changed hospitals. Now the infection and port removal. If I let her into this trial, what if something goes wrong. She can't take it. Her father and I can't either."

Marcy put her hand over Mrs. Baker's. "I know how you feel. You feel like you've lost control. That you don't know enough to make an informed decision. That people who you don't know are telling you to let your child be a guinea pig. That if the medicine doesn't work, then they can walk away but you are left with…" Marcy glanced at Lucy. "You have my word that I'll be there the entire way with you. I'll even give you my private number if you need to talk. That's how strongly I feel about this medicine."

Dylan watched enthralled with Marcy's compassion. For once he saw a glimmer of the girl he'd known. The one who could give as good as she got when pushed into a corner. Dylan looked at her thoughtfully. She spoke as if she'd experienced the same feelings. Had she? He had no right to know, but he couldn't help but be intrigued.

Mrs. Baker looked at Lucy. "Let me talk to my husband."

Marcy nodded. "You should. But don't take too long deciding." She squeezed Mrs. Baker's hand then stood.

Lucy's mother turned to him. "I agree with Dr. Montgomery. I think the best move is to put Lucy in the trial," he said, helping the girl off the exam table.

Lucy went to her mother, who gathered the little girl in her arms. Mrs. Baker said tearfully, "I understand. I just want Lucy to get better."

"That's what we want as well," Marcy said.

"Please let us know in the next day or so what you and Lucy's father decide."

Dylan let Marcy exit the room ahead of him. In the hall, he said softly, "You did good in there. I think they'll make the right decision and join the trial."

"I hope so."

There was a desperation in those few words that he wasn't sure had to do with Lucy joining the trial or more to do with Lucy's parents being able to live with their decision in the months to come.

On the way out of the hospital parking lot that evening Marcy's eyes narrowed as she looked through her car windshield.

Was that Dylan?

His fists rested on his hips in a fighting stance as he glared at the tire of a well-kept antique car.

She'd not seen him since they'd finished clinic rounds. Her interaction with Lucy's mother had been difficult but refreshing. For the first time since Toby had died, she could see a positive. She could clearly understand the pain and fear the family experienced when making decisions that affected their child's life. It was empowering.

She slowly pulled to a stop and opened her window. "Hey, what's going on?"

"My tire is flat again. Second time in three weeks. Apparently the new one isn't any better than the old one."

"Do you have a service?" She studied the listing car.

"Yes, but I'm not gonna mess with this tonight. The car is safe enough here. I'll get a ride home from security and worry about this tomorrow."

"I can take you home."

"Thanks. I'd appreciate that." Dylan picked up the satchel lying on the ground and climbed into the passenger seat, folding his long legs into the small space.

Marcy couldn't help but be aware of his proximity. She shook off the strange sensation and gave the car one last look before she drove toward the parking lot exit. "I had no idea you were into old cars."

"Yeah, that GTO is my pride and joy. I promised myself as soon as I finished med school I'd get one."

"You drive it every day?"

"I do. At least when it doesn't have a flat tire." She smiled at his disgusted sigh. "You need to make a right out of the parking lot. I don't live far from here." They said nothing for a minute. "Where're you staying while you're here?"

"The company rented a furnished apartment. It isn't bad. And not far from here either. I'm learning my way around. It's no joke about Atlanta traffic."

"It's one of the reasons I bought where I did." Dylan leaned back in the seat.

Marcy could feel Dylan watching her. "What're you thinking? You're staring."

He shifted in the seat but continued to watch her. "Go left at the next light. I was wondering how you became so serious. You used to be a lot more easygoing."

"I don't think when working with cancer patients I need to be jolly."

"The next street to the left and third house on the right. Black shutters." His attention went to the road ahead. "You do have a point there."

Marcy pulled into the paved drive. She didn't know what she expected but she was surprised by Dylan's choice of homes. Located in an older neighborhood on a tree-lined street, it looked nothing like an eligible bachelor's house. The homes on his street were redbrick ranch style with large yards, which were beautifully manicured. Dylan's was no exception. He obviously spent his downtime in the yard, or he had a company maintain it. Somehow, he didn't seem like the type of person that would expect someone else to do his work. At the end of his drive and behind the house was a detached garage.

She pulled to a stop next to the back door.

"Home sweet home," Dylan announced as he unfolded himself from the car. He ducked his head back into the car as he stood with the door open. "Have you had dinner? If not, why don't you come in and we can order a pizza?"

Marcy thought a moment. Why shouldn't she? She and Dylan were old friends. It was better than going home to a place that wasn't even hers. She could admit it. She was lonely. She liked him and used to love spending time with him.

Dylan had a great personality. He worked a high-stress job, but he was easygoing. He seemed to be able to separate his personal life from his life inside the hospital. She found it refreshing to be around.

Her entire future had always been planned

out. If not by her parents, then by her. Maybe that was what had drawn her to Dylan in college. He'd seemed to take life as it came instead of manipulating it to fit a plan, as she had. She'd certainly learned the hard way that didn't work. No matter her plans, Toby hadn't survived. It was time she thought less and acted more.

Dylan said nothing, waiting for her answer.

She looked at him. His brown eyes twinkled with warmth and encouragement. "I guess I could do that."

"Great." He came around the car and helped her out before going to the back door. "Come on in." He led her up a couple of steps and opened the door.

She followed him into a large kitchen area with a small dining table sitting next to a window that looked out onto the backyard. The hardwood floors gleamed. Tan curtains hung at the windows. Modern appliances filled the work area. The space had been renovated yet still held its charm.

It was just the type of home she'd always dreamed of having but never had. She and Josh had never made it out of an apartment. She could imagine how nice it would be to have a cup of tea at the table as she watched the morning come alive. To her the room spoke of life being good.

"Come on through. I'll give you the ten-cent tour even though it's only worth about a penny."

Marcy smiled.

Dylan sat his satchel on the counter dividing the small eating area from the work section of the kitchen. "It's nice to have a date that doesn't expect a five-star restaurant."

"This isn't a date but a friendly meal. You might consider changing the type of women you ask out."

He laughed. "You're right on both accounts. Come on into the den where we'll be more comfortable."

They moved through a doorway into a spacious area. She walked around his living area, looking out the front window then running her hand across the back of the worn leather recliner, which was definitely his favorite chair. A large TV was mounted on the wall across the room. A bookcase covering one long wall was filled with books and objects. What she liked best was the back wall that consisted of floor-to-ceiling windows and a French door in the middle. It had obviously been updated with loving care and attention to detail.

Marcy slipped through the French door and stepped out onto a patio made of pavers. An early fall breeze had pushed the humidity of the day away. She took a deep breath and stretched. It felt good to be out of a building. Beneath the trees around the fenced yard was ornamental grass with occasional patches of flowers. It was lovely.

On the patio Dylan had some very masculine wicker furniture with high arms and cushions. The decor suited him as well.

"Would you like to eat out here?"

She jumped at the sound of Dylan's voice, not hearing his approach. "I'd like that. It's nice to get outside when you work in a lab closed off all day. It's a real pleasure to see the outdoors instead of sealed doors and canned air."

"I guess it is."

"I love your flowers, grass…everything." She waved a hand toward the lawn.

"I can't take credit for planting it. I'm just the caretaker of the former owner's work."

"I had no idea you'd be a yard kind of guy."

"I didn't either. I find it therapeutic after a hard day at work. It's so peaceful back here.

If I'm not in the garage tinkering with the car, I spend most of my time out here. Kick off your shoes and enjoy while I go call for the pizza. Make yourself at home."

It didn't take any more invitation than that to have her removing her shoes and pulling off her socks.

He chuckled. "There's a great local pizza place down the road that delivers. So it shouldn't take long. Nothing fancy but I can promise it'll be good. I'll bring us something to drink."

"I didn't come in for you to wait on me." She made a motion to rise.

Dylan waved her down. "I'd let you wait on me, but you don't know where everything is so why don't you let me do it this time?"

She listened to the low rumble of his deep voice as he made the pizza order. There was something soothing about it. An element she shouldn't get used to, but it eased her nerves just the same.

He returned with two large plastic glasses with sports emblems on the side. They were filled to the brim with liquid.

She took a sip and sighed. "This is excellent iced tea."

"Thanks."

Marcy looked around. "You know. I expected you to have a fancy new house and a sports car."

"Remember I am the product of missionaries. I was taught to be much more frugal than that." He settled in a chair.

"Just so you know, I know something about vintage cars. They don't give them away."

He grinned. "Point taken." In a voice meant for the drama of a stage, he continued, "Despite my one obvious, nonrunning weakness I did go into medicine to help people, not for what it would buy me."

She turned serious. "In that we share a common ground."

"I've admitted to my vice. What's yours?" He watched her, waiting.

"I don't know. Let me give that some thought." She knew the answer but telling him would make him think she was crazy. She was driven to save every child who contracted cancer. She wasn't about to tell him that. She couldn't say the words. She'd failed Toby. Had failed herself and her husband. How could she admit that to a person like Dylan?

The doorbell rang. "Then I'll expect a report one day. That must be our pizza."

Half an hour later they were still out on the patio. Marcy was feeling unusually mellow and peaceful. She was grateful that Dylan hadn't pushed her earlier. He was easy company, and easy on the eyes too.

Marcy held up a piece of half-eaten pizza. "This is good stuff."

"Told you so. Best in town."

She took another bite. "You have good taste."

Dylan chuckled. "Thanks, but it's just pizza. You know when you agree on the small things you tend to agree on the bigger ones."

Marcy wrinkled her nose. She wasn't sure about that. As time went by, she and Josh had started to disagree on everything. When it came to Toby, they couldn't seem to agree on anything. Even before Toby became sick, her and Josh's marriage had shown signs of tearing apart. "Are you sure about that?"

"You know you challenged me in college and you're still doing it." He took a long draw on his tea.

Marcy had the distinct feeling he wanted to say more but he didn't. She couldn't help but smile. She remembered those days fondly. They were days before she carried around that knot of loss in her chest. The smell of guilt around her. "We definitely had some good times. You made me laugh. I think Professor Mitchell thought about separating us."

He said in a falsetto voice, "Please stop. You're embarrassing me."

"I wish that were the case, but I think you enjoyed being different from what people expect."

He lifted a shoulder then let it fall. "I care nothing about being a stereotype. And I was different than many of the students. I was on scholarship."

"You weren't stereotypical then and from what I've seen you aren't now. I don't think you need to worry about that ever happening. What's really terrifying for us mere mortals is how well you do everything." She lifted the drink glass. "Even making iced tea."

Dylan watched Marcy with her eyes closed and her face tipped to the late afternoon sun. A golden glow shone around her. It was the most relaxed he'd seen her since she'd been in Atlanta. What was she thinking?

Her manner made him believe she was hiding something. The way she spoke to Mrs. Baker sounded too much like someone who had experienced part of that mother's pain.

When he'd asked about her marrying, she'd said nothing about having a child. If she had one, where was he now? Why was she hiding him? Maybe she just didn't want Dylan to know. Yet why? He wanted to give her friendship. She could trust him with her secrets.

"Why doesn't a nice guy like you have a wife or a girlfriend?"

He was shaken out of his thoughts. "Maybe because I'm too nice."

Marcy huffed. "There's no such thing. Over half the nursing staff has a crush on you. At least half the female population of your patients do too. Regardless of age."

"I could ask you the same thing. Did you know I had a crush on you in college?"

Her eyes opened. "You did?"

Dylan gave her a narrow-eyed "you must be kidding" look. "You don't remember me asking you to go for pizza? You turned me down."

Marcy's mouth twisted and her brows rose. "I did?"

"You did. That's when I learned you had a boyfriend. I've always wondered why you didn't mention him sooner." He crossed his ankle over his knee.

"I kind of liked you too. I guess I didn't

want to ruin the fun we were having by telling you about Josh."

"You broke my heart." The words were direct, but soft; just the truth.

Marcy sat up. Her voice held concern. "Dylan, I didn't mean to."

"I know." Dylan met her gaze. "When I found out you had a boyfriend, I made sure to hide how I felt."

She clutched her hands in her lap. "I'm sorry. I wouldn't have hurt you for anything."

"You didn't know. I shouldn't have even brought it up. That was a long time ago and we were kids."

"I just want you to know I liked you more than I knew I should. I wouldn't let myself think about that. You know I looked for you at graduation. You said you were coming but I didn't see you. Did you decide not to go?"

He hadn't planned to attend the ceremony. She'd talked him into doing so. "I was there. I saw you."

"Why didn't you come say hello?" she asked, continuing to watch him.

"Because I saw you run into some guy's arms. I didn't want to intrude."

She leaned her head back on the chair cushion and closed her eyes "Yeah. That was Josh.

The boyfriend turned ex-husband. He surprised me by showing up. He was jealous of you."

Dylan sat forward. "Jealous of me? Why would he be?"

"Because I talked about you so much." The words tumbled out while her eyes remained closed.

Dylan didn't know what to say, so he said nothing. He had no doubt he hadn't been popular with the guy. "Yeah. He recognized I liked you more than I should. In hindsight I should have paid attention to the fact I could have those feelings for someone else. I might have saved Josh and me some heartache." She continued to talk as if Dylan weren't there. As if from a far-off place. "We had our life all planned out. It was going to be perfect. But life doesn't really work that way, does it? All perfect and easy. The unexpected comes along and pushes you off the road into the grass and dirt."

Dylan didn't comment right away. "No, it doesn't. We can plan and wish for something, and it never comes your way." Like him having a family close at Christmas, or a birthday cake on his actual birthday not months later.

Or a friend that didn't have to suffer with cancer. "I'm sorry if I made life difficult for you."

She looked at him then placed her hand over his. "It wasn't anything you did. What went wrong between Josh and me was all there when I was in college. I just didn't choose to see it. Or I was too young to. We were small town high school sweethearts that everyone thought would marry. We didn't disappoint. The problem was what we had as kids didn't work in the grown-up world."

Dylan said nothing, waiting on her to share more. Instead, a few minutes later Marcy's soft snoring reached his ears. He didn't have the heart to wake her just yet. She'd been keeping long hours. Too many of them in his opinion.

Boundaries where his work was concerned had always been a priority. He wanted to enjoy his life, not just fill it with obligations as his father had. Even if it was worthwhile work. Like tonight. Her hand still rested on his, and he left it there, enjoying her touch and the company he rarely had. It felt right having Marcy at his house. He'd give her a few more minutes to nap.

When Marcy slapped at a mosquito, he

said, "Hey, sleepyhead, let's go in before you get eaten up."

"I'm sorry. I didn't mean to fall sleep on you. It's so lovely out I just drifted off."

"It's more likely from the long hours you're keeping. You work harder and longer than three people put together."

"I want to get the trial right." She stretched.

He watched, entranced. She moved with such grace.

"I'm not worried about the trial. I'm concerned about you and your health. You keep a mean pace." She picked up her shoes after stuffing her socks into them. Gathering her glass, she held the door for him.

"You killing yourself won't save others' lives." Dylan stacked the plates, picked up his glass and took them to the kitchen. He placed them in the sink.

Marcy joined him, putting her glass in beside his. "Still my work needs doing."

"Yes, it does. But not taking care of yourself might mean you make a mistake. You don't want that."

"You do know I'm a big girl and decide those things on my own?"

"Hey," he said, reaching out to touch her. "I didn't mean to overstep. I apologize. You're right it's none of my business. A balance of work and play is just a pet peeve of mine. I shouldn't put that off on you."

"I understand. I'd better get going. Thanks for the pizza. It was great catching up." She stepped toward the kitchen table where she'd left her purse.

"It's not too late. Would you like to watch a movie before you go?"

She looked unsure for a moment then said, "I don't think so. I really do have some numbers I need to look at early in the morning before some patients come in. I better call it a night."

Monday morning Dylan entered the hospital looking forward to seeing Marcy. He'd not seen her Friday because of an off campus meeting. During the weekend he'd thought of calling her several times but had stopped himself. He had the sense Marcy wanted to keep him at arm's length. Or was it everyone? She wasn't the same person he'd known in college. There was a shell around her that hadn't been there before.

Either way he had no interest in being left behind again. Marcy had done it innocently, but his ex-fiancée had done it brutally by leaving him for an old boyfriend weeks before their wedding. No, he wasn't interested in having his teeth kicked in again. Especially not by a blast from his past whom he hadn't even dated. They should just remain friends. Maybe he was remembering the past too fondly?

Dylan smiled. Marcy had acted as if she liked his home. He'd enjoyed having her there. Oddly she fit. Too well and too quickly for his comfort. She added a warmth he hadn't known was missing—until he saw her again. He didn't make a habit of inviting women to his home. It was his place to decompress.

He stopped by his office to check his messages and took a half hour seeing to them. When Marcy showed up he had already started with his first case.

She quickly joined him and pulled a stool up next to the patient. "Good morning, everyone."

The mother and daughter returned the greeting.

Dylan continued to do his examination, but he couldn't deny the pleased beat of his heart at the sight of Marcy. It was nice to see the happy look on her face. She'd become more relaxed in the clinic over the last week. That shouldn't matter, after all she'd only be there for a few weeks, but somehow it did matter.

They continued around the room, seeing all the patients. Marcy spoke to each one, listening to the parents and their sick children. Every so often she placed her hand on a parent's hand or shoulder giving reassurance, as if they were sharing a bond. One he didn't understand.

Having finished with clinic and expecting a light afternoon, it was a good time to move Marcy's office.

"Hey, since we're done here, why don't we get your office moved?"

An unsure look filled her eyes. "Doing that really isn't necessary."

"But I think it is. I'm going to insist. You've been in that rathole long enough and I have plenty of room in my office to share. With the hours you've been keeping you need somewhere comfortable to work."

She shifted her weight. Today she wore her hair down and pulled back on the sides. She didn't look as stark and sad as she had the first day he'd seen her. The lines around her eyes had eased. "I must admit it's more crowded than I imagined. The interruptions are certainly greater than I thought they would be."

"Then it's settled. I'll call down and see if I can get somebody from our maintenance staff to help with the desk. I think you and I can handle the rest."

Marcy smiled. "Then I'll go started packing up."

"Give me five minutes. I'll be right behind you." Dylan pulled his phone out of his pocket, ridiculously pleased that she'd agreed to his plan.

A young man arrived from Maintenance half an hour later. Between him and Dylan, they managed to get Marcy's desk down the hall and into place without too much difficulty. Dylan had it placed at an angle giving her as much space as possible.

The man left.

Marcy entered with her arms filled with files, books and a laptop. She looked around. "This reminds me of when we had to use that old lab after Wilson created that sulfur mess during an experiment."

Dylan chuckled. "He did make a mess. Then the class had to divide up into all those smaller rooms to work. We could hardly move around." He'd loved every minute of being that close to Marcy. "Let me have some of that before you drop it," he offered, rushing toward her.

The bulk of the material was all that stood between them. He was close enough that he could smell the spring scent of her shampoo. His gaze met hers as he slid his arms along her bare ones to support the pile. Marcy blinked then released the items into his hands.

Dylan stepped back, clearing his throat. His mind shouldn't be going to how wonderful her skin felt or how bright her eyes were or, worse, how kissable her full mouth looked. He had to put a stop to those thoughts. He wasn't a college kid with a crush anymore. Getting involved with Marcy again wasn't what he needed in his life. Dylan feared she could too easily break his heart again. He set the pile on the corner of her desk. "I'll…uh… let you get settled. I have a couple of consults to see about."

He headed out of the office without a backward look. Being nice just might get him in trouble.

Marcy looked up from the work she was doing on the laptop when Dylan entered. He dropped into his chair behind his desk. They had been sharing an office for a couple of days. During that time, she'd seen little of him. Most of their interactions happened outside the too-close working environment. He had respected her space by not disturbing her when they were in the room together but that didn't mean she wasn't aware of him nearby.

He'd only clicked a few keys when his phone rang. "Yeah. I can be there in a few minutes." He hung up. Pushing back from the desk, Dylan said, "This consult case has nothing to do with your trial but it's unusual. Would you like to go with me?"

She looked at the work on the computer screen. Closing the laptop, she stood. "I'd like a break."

"Good. We're going to the cardiology floor."

"Since when do they call Oncology for help?"

Dylan headed for the stairs. "Today apparently. The patient has an extremely low platelet count."

"I see. Handling the immune system the cancer department is the most familiar with."

Dylan grinned, the gleam in his chocolate-brown \\\\\\eyes sending her pulse racing. "You're a smart cookie."

"Thanks. Coming from you that's nice to

hear. I guess the cardiologist wants to see if you have any ideas about what's causing the drop." She hurried to keep up with him.

"That's it." Dylan pushed through the door to the stairs' then climbed.

Marcy followed him onto the next floor, They stopped at the nurses' station, where he checked in before going to the room number he was given. Dylan knocked and they entered. A young man in his late teens lay in the bed. A woman sat in a chair nearby.

"I'm Dr. Nelson. Are you Ryan?"

"Yep." The boy continued to watch the TV.

"Dr. Connors asked me to come by to see you. This is Dr. Montgomery," Dylan said, indicating her. "Do you mind if we have a look at your chest?"

"You want to see the spots, don't you?" Ryan lifted his shirt without any hesitation, showing an old incision down the center of his chest. His nonchalant action common for children who'd been in and out of the hospital most of their lives.

She and Dylan stepped closer. This was an unusual case for an oncologist. Marcy had to admit she was intrigued.

"I understand you had a heart transplant some time ago." Dylan looked at the boy.

"Yeah." Ryan focused on the game he was playing.

"Sixteen years," the woman sitting in a nearby chair said.

"That's a long time." Dylan nodded.

"He's recently had an aorta replacement and pacemaker," the woman said.

Dylan studied the red dots on the boy's chest. "Did the petechiae show up before or after that?"

"The what?" The boy looked perplexed. Dylan had his attention now. Ryan glanced at the woman who must be his mother.

"The red spots," Dylan said without taking his attention away from the boy's chest.

"Oh. After the pacemaker." Ryan's hand went to his chest.

"May I touch a moment?" Dylan asked.

"Sure." The boy lay still.

Dylan pushed on a spot. The area around the spot turned white but the spot returned to the skin when Dylan removed his fingertip. "Have you ever had platelet issues before?"

"No," the mother replied. She rose and came to stand beside the bed.

"I'm afraid they're very low. I'm going to order another round of packed blood cells to see if that'll help. If not, we have a medicine I think we need to try."

Ryan nodded.

The mother asked, "When will you start?"

Dylan gave her a reassuring look. "As soon as I can order it."

"Thanks," she said, sounding tired.

Marcy recognized the note of worry in the woman's voice because at one time she'd been that mother.

Dylan gave Ryan's mother a reassuring smile and stepped out into the hall. Marcy followed him.

"He has thrombocytopenic purpura," Marcy said.

"He does."

"You think he's going to need IVIG."

His mouth thinned. "I do."

She knew IVIG was an anticancer treatment and would cost the patient thousands of dollars per infusion. But it looked as if it might be the only way to increase the young man's platelet count. He couldn't go about life or have another procedure with his platelet count so low. He could bleed to death. There was no choice, just as there hadn't been for the treatment Toby had received.

Her heart tightened. "What's your plan if the platelets don't work?"

"I'll have him come in for IVIG infusions once a week for three weeks and see how it goes." Dylan paused. "Ryan's platelets are dangerously low but keeping him here won't make things better. Being in the hospital just increases his chance of an infection. You know the saying, 'you get sick in the hospital.'"

Marcy nodded. "That's generally the truth."

They started down the hall. Marcy faced a mother with a baby in her arms about the age Toby had been when he'd become sick. She clenched her hands. On one level, she was getting better; she didn't want to run. But after seeing the teen and now this her nerves were strung tight. This is why she belonged in a lab, where it was safer.

"Thanks for bringing me along. I better get back to work." She hurried ahead of Dylan and through the double doors. Marcy caught Dylan's surprised glance but kept walking.

CHAPTER FOUR

FOR DYLAN THE next few days moved eternally slowly while at the same time flew by. He had adjusted to sharing his office with Marcy. Sort of. More than once he found himself stopping by for something he normally would have let wait just to see what Marcy was doing. When she wasn't with him, she spent the time seeing patients in the office, working on her laptop and talking on the phone.

They were slowly rebuilding the comradery they'd enjoyed in college. At first he wasn't sure it was possible. Sharing a joke, a memory or a laugh over something that had happened during the day had improved their relationship. Now he was sure that Marcy was hiding something but that wasn't his business. She was entitled to her privacy. He didn't want people prying into his life, so why should he do it to her. Still, he couldn't stop his curiosity.

On Friday afternoon Dylan hit the final computer key in his email response and huffed. Why did he always get this job? Yet he couldn't say no.

She looked up from her laptop screen. "Something wrong?"

"Marcy, do you think you have time to help me with something?" Maybe new eyes on the project would help.

"Like what?" She sounded hesitant.

"In a few weeks the cancer caregivers are giving the Care Ball to raise money for new equipment."

"Cancer caregivers?" Marcy raised her brows, giving her a cute inquiring expression.

He had her complete attention. "They're the volunteers who support the pediatric oncology department. Do fundraisers."

"Okay. So how can I help?" With her elbows on the desk and head resting on her hands, her gorgeous green eyes searched his face.

"I've been asked to give a presentation about the department at the ball. To 'showcase it' were the words. They left it up to me to decide what I do, but it must raise money.

I hate doing this sort of stuff. Inspirational speeches aren't my thing. Please help me. I'll take any ideas."

Marcy wore a half smile. "Begging and whining will get you everywhere. Let me think about it. I have the first part of the trial settled so I have a little more time."

"I'm desperate enough to take any time you can give. Just don't think too long. They want this in four weeks." He was completely out of his depth with no idea of where to start.

"Ooh, that's a short time. That'll be about the time I leave. Do you have anything in mind?"

He shrugged. "I can always stand up there and give statistics along with how important the work we do is."

Marcy put her hand over her mouth and patted it as if stifling a yawn.

He glared at her with a grin. "Why don't you tell me how you really feel?"

She looked away from him, the expression in her eyes thoughtful. "I think you should showcase the patients."

When Dylan started to speak, she raised a hand. "I don't mean anything to sensational-ize them or be insensitive. I know how you like to protect them."

"So what do you have in mind?" He perched on the corner of her desk, slowly swinging a leg as he listened.

"I don't know yet. Maybe pictures around the room? Or videos of the patients? But that's all been done. You want something that will grab them. You know them all so well. Outside of cancer, do they have anything in common?"

"Not really. They're different ages. Live in different parts of the city. Some outside the city. I don't know."

She pursed her mouth. "There has to be something."

"They like to sing, rap. You heard them the other day. The one they made up about me was pretty funny."

Marcy's eyes brightened as she pointed her finger at him. "That's it. If we can get some of the patients to come to the ball and be among the people, and then do a song. Like one of those crowds…"

"You mean a flash mob?"

"Yeah. Make it look impromptu. They can rap something about being in the hospital or taking chemo like they did the other day. Those attending will love it. It would showcase how well the patients are doing. That despite what they're going through, they're still full of life."

Dylan looked at her for a moment. "That sounds great. The committee will love it." Before he knew what he was doing, he'd pulled her into his arms and kissed her. Realizing what he'd done, he let her go and put the desk between them. "I'm sorry. I got excited. I shouldn't have done that. You're wonderful."

She watched him with wide eyes. "I'm glad you like the idea. Now you just have to get the children and parents to cooperate."

"I'm better at that than being the idea guy. Thanks again, Marcy."

She gave a slight nod. "You're welcome."

"Don't think you're done. I'll still need your help to get it all organized."

"Are you asking or telling?" Marcy sounded unsure.

He gave her a pleading look. "Uh, I'm asking. I promise, I'm asking."

She grinned.

He returned it. "We're going to make a great team. The kids will be the stars of the show as they should be."

A week later on a Saturday afternoon Marcy checked off another item on the list she and

Dylan had made to prepare for the Care Ball. He'd insisted she come to his house to work on the details and plans. They'd put together schedules and decided on how they wanted the children to enter the room.

They had spent the last week talking to the patients and parents encouraging them to be involved with the Care Ball. They still had a few more to talk to on Monday but all in all they were encouraged.

Robby, the lead rapper, had been the patient they really had to get on board. He took more convincing than Marcy expected.

"Dr. Nelson, we're just having fun here. No one wants to hear us."

Dylan had scooted his rolling stool closer. "I think you'd be surprised. You and the others are great. Do you think we stop and clap around here just because we have nothing else to do?"

The teen had shrugged. "I haven't really thought about it. We're just passing time."

"I get that, but we need you to make this work. I'll tell you what, you and the kids come up with whatever song you want to do. Practice it. Just one. See what you think."

"I guess we could."

"Thanks, Robby. I knew I could count on you."

Marcy had to respect Dylan for nudging Robby because she knew he was concerned about them not overdoing it. After all they were all taking chemo treatments.

By the end of the week Robby had agreed. The other patients and their parents were eager to help after that.

Dylan went to the back of his house but soon returned. "We've been at this awhile. Let's take a break and go do something fun."

"I really should go to the hospital and check some numbers." Marcy closed her laptop.

Dylan's shoulders sagged. "Come on, Marcy. You work all the time. You can take an afternoon off if you want to. Especially on the weekend. I promise you'll like what I have in mind."

Really, her work was caught up, but after their kiss she felt more aware of Dylan than ever. It had been a quick meeting of lips, but the action had made her come alive like nothing had in a long time. Truthfully, she wanted him to do it again. What would it be like if he really meant it?

"I guess I could go for a little while."

Dylan placed a hand on her shoulder.

"Good. Then let's go." He started toward the door. "Come on. Time's wasting. We'll take my car."

A few minutes later she gave his car a dubious look. "Are you making any guarantees I won't have to walk home today?"

Dylan squared his shoulders. His voice filled with false hurt. "I don't appreciate my dates questioning my automobile."

At the word *date* her gaze quickly turned to him. Marcy smiled and met his laughing brown eyes. Her stomach gave a small flip. "Actually, I was just kidding."

What was happening to her? Was she flirting with Dylan? She hadn't had interest in a man in so long she couldn't imagine trying to flirt. "I'm looking forward to riding in it."

He grinned. "You'll appreciate the fact that it's fall instead of summer since there's no air-conditioning."

She laughed. "I'll make a note of that."

He opened and held the passenger car door. She settled into the seat with the fanfare of a woman testing its comfort. Running her hands along the leather upholstery of the door, she studied it.

The fleeting thought of what it would feel like to have Dylan's hand run over her skin made her breath catch. She shook her head. She shouldn't let those thoughts happen. Hopefully she'd made the right decision by going with him today.

As Dylan pulled into the main road, Marcy rolled the window down far enough that her hair blew around her face.

"Which would you like to do most—go to a plantation house or see a museum or take a train ride? Or we could go up the sky lift to the top of the mountain?"

She turned to gape at him. "Where're we going that you have all those choices?"

Dylan glanced at her before he changed lanes. "Stone Mountain. Ever heard of it?"

"No, but I think I'd like to go up on top of the mountain."

"Then that's what we'll do." Dylan followed the signs to the parking area for the sky lift.

"It's huge." Marcy looked up at the white-and-gray stone soaring from the ground. "What kind of mountain is this? I was expecting trees on top of it."

Dylan chuckled. "There are trees but around it. Stone Mountain is what is called a monadnock. It's when the hard rock remains as the ground around it erodes."

Less than an hour later they were in a cable car riding up the side of the huge stone. Marcy stood at the window, looking out. Dylan moved in close but not touching. She felt his warmth beside her. "This is beautiful. Amazing."

Soon they stopped at the top and stepped from the car. They walked over to the rail and looked out at the flat top of the stone, then past that to the view beyond. Dylan moved over to a sign posted on the wall. "We're up 825 feet and you can see sixty miles in any direction."

Marcy shifted to another area. "Can we see the hospital from here?"

Dylan stepped next to her. He raised an arm and pointed. "It's right down there. The sand-colored building next to the blue one."

"Where?" She moved in close enough that her back touched his chest and she followed the line of sight down his arm. His aftershave smelled spicy, and it took everything she had not to give in to the temptation to lean back into the warmth of his body. "I think I see it now."

Dylan shifted away.

She immediately missed his contact. "Atlanta really does have a beautiful skyline."

"It does. I like living here."

"I can understand why." She continued to look out at the city.

They spent the next thirty minutes wandering around looking from different view spots before taking the cable car down. By that time the sun had\ moved lower in the sky.

"Are you getting hungry?" Dylan asked.

"I'm all right for now."

They strolled toward the car.

Dylan said, "Are you're interested in staying for the laser show?"

"Now, that sounds interesting. I've never been to something like that. What do we do?"

A car backed out in front of them and he took her hand, directing her out of the way. She didn't pull away. It was calming to have her hand clasped in his larger one. As if he was protecting her like he did his patients. Even with the small amount of attention Dylan had shown her she could only imagine how comforting it would be under the umbrella of his love. Safe. What had her thinking about that?

"We don't do anything but watch. They shine large bright-colored lights on the curved side of the mountain and pair it with music."

"That sounds fun." Her pulse picked up.

She would be spending another evening with Dylan. This wasn't like her. It would be easy to get carried away with being around him, which she couldn't let happen. What would he think of her if he learned about her failure with Toby? That she'd missed her son's illness until it was too late, and he'd died because of her. Would Dylan trust her again? With his patients? In his life? No, she had to stay away from him. She slipped her hand from his as soon as the danger passed.

"I'd hoped you'd like the idea. I called ahead for a catered meal. We need to move the car to a closer parking lot and get the blanket."

She stopped walking and looked at him. "You planned all this?"

"Well, yes, but I was nowhere sure you'd come or stay. Work is all you think about, except for the Care Ball, but then it's part of work too. I wanted us to do something together that was just for us."

Marcy smiled. Warmth flowed through her. When was the last time someone had wanted to spend time with just her? She liked the idea too much. "I'd love a picnic."

A smile reached his eyes as if she'd given

him a present. "Good. Because that's just what we're having."

An hour later, with a blanket under his arm, Dylan carried a picnic basket they had picked up from a van in the parking lot. They made their way to the wide grassy mound in front of a large sculpture on the side of the mountain.

Dylan spread the blanket on the ground and they took a seat, stretching out their legs. "Are you ready to eat or would you like to wait for a little bit?"

Marcy lifted her face to the last of the late afternoon sun. "I think I'd like to wait. It's been a nice afternoon, Dylan. Thank you for insisting I come."

"Insist?" He gave her a shocked look as if she'd hurt his feelings.

She grinned. "Yes, I think that's an accurate word for it. But I'm glad you did."

"I'm glad you came too. I hope you haven't worried too much about work."

"I haven't. I needed somebody to push me out of the hole my head has been in." She'd never spoken truer words. The reality that she'd stopped living when Toby died suddenly swamped her.

"Are you okay? You have a strange look on your face."

"I'm fine." Yet she wasn't. Her entire world had just tilted but she couldn't let on to Dylan.

While they sat there, other people settled in around them with their blankets and chairs.

Dylan served their meals of fried chicken, rolls, a small green salad and a brownie for dessert. Along with that, Dylan had brought a bottle of wine. They made small talk about the day as they ate.

"Thanks, Dylan. I really needed this." A long purple light reflected brilliantly off the granite rock. Marcy asked, "Is this the light show?"

"Yes." As a yellow light was added he cleared away their dinner. He held up the wine bottle. "Would you like one last glass?"

"No thanks." Marcy sat with her arms wrapped around her knees. "I don't want to miss anything."

Dylan chuckled, corked the bottle and set it aside. He lay on his side with his ankles crossed and his head in his palm to watch the show.

Over the next hour Marcy became enthralled with the bright lights against the mountain set to music. After one song she leaned over and whispered, "I know this is silly for a grown-up, but this is a lot of fun."

Dylan grinned. "I don't think it's silly. I'm glad you're having a good time."

As dark settled around them the air cooled. Marcy rubbed her arms as she wrapped them around her waist. Dylan moved in closer, placing an arm over her shoulder, bringing her into his side. "I'm sorry I don't have anything warmer to offer."

"It's okay. I'm warm now." She was. Warmer than she'd been in years. It had been too long since she had real human contact. It felt nice to have Dylan caring for her. More than nice; her whole body seemed to sparkle along with the light show.

She watched the rest of the show snuggled against Dylan's side. They often sang along to the music. She could get used to this, too easily. And she could get too attached to Dylan. Something she mustn't let happen. It wasn't healthy for her or him.

With the show over, they gathered their belongings, then walked to the car. Dylan turned up the heat inside, but she missed the warmth of his touch. "That really was fun. Thank you for taking me. You're a good guy, Dylan Nelson."

Marcy deliberately made it sound like they were just friends. It was safer that way.

"Thanks. I'm glad you think so. You've never done anything like that before?"

"If I did, it was a long time ago. I've pretty much spent all my time working."

"You should take more downtime into your life. You're going to burn out if you aren't careful. You need to let your mind turn off."

He had no idea. "I know but it's harder to do than you think." Work kept her memories and guilt at bay. Work was her mechanism for survival. For finding a cure to cancer or at least something that prevented families from experiencing what she went through. "Am I all that bad? I don't remember asking for your opinion on my life." It came out more harshly than she intended.

"I'm sorry. You're right. Your life is none of my business. Forgive me for offering advice that wasn't asked for. I do have that habit."

Neither of them said anything more as he turned into his drive, but tension hovered between them. She climbed out of his car and headed toward her own. "Thanks for the evening, Dylan. I had a great time. I'm glad you insisted I go. I did need it."

"I'm glad you went too." He waited beside the steps to his back door as she left his drive.

If she'd had hope for a good evening kiss, that had gotten lost in their last conversation. And that was probably a good thing.

Tuesday, Dylan went into the hospital with his mind firmly on what he had to do that day. He'd spent too much time over the last few days rethinking his and Marcy's last exchange. He had no business offering advice about how she spent her time when he had his own issues.

His father had called again and left a message asking if Dylan had made a decision about coming to work with him in the medical mission. Sometime today Dylan would have to return that call. He wasn't looking forward to the discussion. He wanted to help his father, but Dylan liked his work here and living in Atlanta. He had no desire to move around. Stability, building a life in one place, appealed to him.

Yet not wanting to disappoint his father still tugged at him. In a strange way the fact he'd shared little of his father's life growing up made Dylan want to get some of that time back as an adult. He wasn't sure what a psychiatrist would say about that. He resented his parents for putting him last in their lives. Just for once he'd like to hear they wanted what he wanted. He feared that day might never come.

"Hey," Marcy said as she came in the door. "I didn't know if you knew that Lucy is here for her port."

"Yeah. I'm on my way. I checked my schedule earlier and saw her name on the list." He read his last email.

"Do you mind if I observe?" Marcy put her purse away in the desk and lay her laptop down.

The technology went everywhere with her. She was always prepared to do work. Something she did too much of. "Not at all. In fact, I would've been surprised if you didn't."

Twenty minutes later Lucy lay sedated on the table in the port lab as Dylan prepared to insert the port. Marcy stood across from him. He felt more than saw her unwavering gaze on what he was doing.

She'd come into the lab a few minutes after him, having stopped to speak to Lucy's mother when they passed her in the hall. There was something Marcy was able to offer Mrs. Baker that he couldn't. Maybe it was just because they were female. Marcy was good for his department. He could already tell the difference she made, and it had nothing to do with the new drug trial.

They finished the procedure in under half an hour and walked to the waiting room to speak to Lucy's mom. Dylan stood but Marcy sat beside the mother. "Lucy is doing great. She'll be sleepy today, and maybe a little sore, but she should be good to go tomorrow. Do all the things you did last time for the port. We'll start her chemo on Wednesday. They'll give you the appointment time up front. I know Dr. Montgomery has spoken to you about the TM13, but do you have any other questions?"

Mrs. Baker shook her head. "I don't think so. I'm just ready for all this to be over and for Lucy to be better."

Marcy touched her arm. "Just take one day at a time. You'll get through it. I promise."

Lucy's mother gave her a weak smile. "I hope so."

"Just know that Dr. Nelson is the best and he'll take good care of Lucy."

Dylan liked hearing a vote of confidence directed at him from Marcy. "Then we'll see you week after next to start chemo."

Mrs. Baker nodded as Marcy rose. "You have my card. Call if you need to talk."

He and Marcy said their goodbyes and walked toward the lab.

"You were really good with Lucy's mother. Giving her your number was nice. Have you ever thought about getting out of the lab and working with the cancer families? Using your knowledge outside the glass. There are hospitals that have those types of programs led by doctors. You would be great at it."

Marcy gave him a shocked look. "I can't imagine not doing the work I do."

"It wasn't always your dream to be a researcher?"

"No, it was just my dream to help people. How about you? How did you become a doctor?"

"It was always the plan. When we knew each other before, I wasn't sure it was going to work out. I took a couple of years off to work between college and med school. I needed money to live on. My parents didn't have that kind of money for school. My father is a doctor, and he's always wanted me to work with him on the mission field. I always felt there were other places I could serve where I could help people. Lately he's been pressuring me to join him."

She grabbed his arm, surprising him. "Are you seriously considering it?"

Dylan shook his head, trying to ignore the feel of her hand on his skin. "No. My place is here. I just have to make him understand that."

"Then why don't you tell him that?" Marcy's gaze was intense.

"Because I don't want to hurt his feelings. I guess it's just easier to dodge that conversation." What he didn't want to admit was that he'd found and created a home without them. He didn't want to live as his parents had. He liked his life. After not belonging anywhere, he'd found the place where he fit.

When she dropped his arm, he stopped and leaned against the wall. "Because there are few doctors in developing countries. Dad's getting older and with no one to take his place..."

She glowered at him in disbelief. "But you've put down roots here. You do great work here. Your patients depend on you too. They deserve to know you'll be here when you're needed."

"I know but my father has always believed I would become part of the family business. Despite them not being around while I was growing up, he expects me to join him." Dylan tried to keep the bitterness out of his voice but failed.

A look of disbelief made Marcy's eyes darker. "I think it would be a shame for you to leave what you have established here. It feels wrong!"

Dylan watched her curiously. Marcy sure was invested in his future when she would be leaving it in a few weeks.

"I think you're right square in the middle of the family business here in Atlanta." She stopped short of stomping a foot.

"Why would you say that?"

"You're a doctor with compassion like I've never seen before. You're helping people. Helping families. Helping children. How's that different from being a missionary. It's not the country that matters but the needs."

Why did her words ease the heaviness he carried? "I've never really thought of it like that. I always saw me not working in a developing nation as disappointing my parents and not using my skills to the best advantage."

"I'd be surprised if you aren't using them to their best advantage. I have a feeling anybody you care about you care deeply for."

Why was she so adamant about him staying? She'd be gone soon, and they wouldn't see each other again for a long time, if ever. The thought stung him more than he would like. "What about you? What happens after the trial is over? Will you disappear inside a lab again?"

"It's not a prison, you know. I'll start on the development of a new, better drug until there's a cure."

Dylan pursed his lips and shrugged, feigning indifference. "I just think you might be missing your calling."

The sound of rapping lured them both to the Infusion Room.

Dylan grinned. Robby was beatboxing and the others were adding phrases as the group, all hooked to IV lines, continued to keep rhythm. Marcy came to stand beside him.

The song came to an end and Robby picked up again. "Dr. Montgomery can give you a summary."

Lizzy, a girl of nine, added, "Anytime, with what is on her mind."

Dylan looked at Marcy. There was a smile on her face but her eyes glistened.

When the group had finished she clapped her hands enthusiastically. "That was wonderful. Even if it was about me. You guys will be stars at the ball. If you think you'll have any trouble getting there, please let Dr. Nelson or me know. We'll be glad to come get you."

"Remember, if you're not feeling up to it also let us know that. Your health is top priority," Dylan added.

Marcy turned to Dylan and said for his ears only. "How could you even think about leaving this behind?"

CHAPTER FIVE

THURSDAY MORNING, MARCY GROANED. She'd been at Atlanta Children's four weeks. Days that had changed her life.

During the day she'd spent too much time thinking about Dylan. He'd started to slip beyond her locked gate of emotions to make her want someone again. Not just someone—him. More than once she'd hoped he'd call. More than once she'd thought of calling him. It was thrilling and disconcerting to have these feelings again.

She had no desire to mislead Dylan. He certainly needed someone who wasn't scared to love. What could she ever offer him? She promised she'd never let herself care about anyone again. Having lost so much in her life already she couldn't afford to take a chance on losing someone else. More than that she couldn't trust herself to be what he needed. What if she failed him?

She went through the motions of the day pushing thoughts of Dylan away. It was the middle of the afternoon when she remembered Ryan, the heart transplant teen was due to come in for his first treatment for low platelets. She went to the clinic in search of Dylan and the boy. She found them in a small room off the main area.

The lights had been lowered. The boy sat in a cushioned recliner, looking at the TV hanging on the wall. The sports channel played. A nurse worked with the IV already in the boy's arm while Dylan held an electric pad in his hands.

Wearing a solemn expression, he looked at Ryan. "How're you feeling?"

"Fine." Ryan didn't take his gaze off the TV.

Dylan glanced at Ryan's mother, who nodded.

Ryan and his mom acted as if they were taking the situation in stride. Marcy questioned whether they really understood how bad Ryan's condition was. Or if they had just been through so much this setback was another issue in a long line of them. Either way Marcy wished she had their peace.

Marcy had been amazed after reading Ryan's chart at how he'd managed to grow to a teenager. Now he faced another ongoing issue. His mother had come close to losing her child several times. They both wore a smile of greeting when Marcy spoke to them. How did they manage to endure?

Dylan stepped to Ryan's side. "We're gonna give you some medicine called gamma globulin. It's to help increase your platelet count. May I see your chest?"

Ryan lifted his shirt.

Marcy moved to the other side of the lounge chair.

"These small red dots are caused by the platelet issue. It indicates bleeding under the skin. These petechiae should disappear as your platelet count increases. We must get your platelet count up to keep you healthy. You've got to be very careful not to hurt yourself or cause bleeding until we do."

Ryan nodded, but focused on the TV again.

"You'll need to come in once a week for three sessions in the hope we can increase your count. I must admit the sessions can be hours long. We can only put the medicine in as fast as your body will tolerate it."

Ryan nodded.

Marcy looked at his mother, who sat on the edge of the chair, her attention on Dylan.

He continued, "I'll be checking on other patients and then come back and see you. There'll be a nurse here with you the entire time. Are we good?"

"We're good," Ryan said to Dylan.

He looked at Ryan's mom.

"We're good," she said.

Dylan left the room and Marcy followed.

"Have you done this procedure before?" Marcy asked his retreating back.

He turned to her. "Several times but all on cancer kids. I've never done it on a heart transplant patient."

"Do you have any idea what to expect?" She watched him closely.

Dylan pursed his lips. "All are educated guesses on this type of patient. You never know with the immunosuppressed."

"You have a great bedside manner. I wish I had that talent." His manners were good in more ways than one.

He studied her a moment, then said, "I think you do. I think you just fear using it."

Dylan walked off. Somehow, she felt as if she'd been scolded.

Later, on her way to the office, she passed a small consult room. Ryan's mother sat there alone with her head down. Her hands rested in her lap. Marcy considered walking on, but something stopped her. She knocked. Ryan's mother looked up and Marcy entered.

"Is there a problem? Is Ryan having a reaction to the medicine?"

She shook her head. "No, I just needed a moment away."

"Then I'll leave you alone," Marcy said, moving to leave.

"No, please stay."

"Is there something I can do to help?" Marcy took a seat unsure where that question had come from. She never asked it before. But then she'd not been in a hospital setting dealing with patients on a regular basis since medical school.

Thankfully Ryan's mother didn't act as if she noticed Marcy's discomfort. Instead she continued talking. "Sometimes I just can't watch what's happening to Ryan."

"He and your family have been through a lot."

"Yeah, it just seems to always be one more thing, then one more thing." The woman's words came out weary.

"I can tell Ryan is a fighter. And so are you."

"I don't know. Some days I put up a good front for him. I don't know if he does or not. We just do what we can and live the best we can every day."

Marcy quit doing that when Toby died. "That's to be admired."

"I don't think I do anything special. I just do what must be done. I'm just a parent who loves her kid. You just do."

Hadn't Marcy done that and not made any difference? "Do you ever feel like you don't do enough?"

"Every day. I think even parents with children who are perfectly healthy feel like they don't do enough. I do the best I can with what knowledge I have at the time."

Had Marcy done that? She had, to the best of her ability.

"We can't do any more. After all, we're just human," Ryan's mother said, drawing a circle on the table with her fingertip.

Marcy had never thought about it that way. She had loved Toby. She had done all she could with the knowledge she had. The problem was she couldn't do enough.

"His dad and I make sure he knows every day that if something ever does happen to him, his mom and dad loved and wanted him to have the best life possible."

Hadn't she and Josh done that? She believed they had. "I'm sure Ryan does know that."

The woman gave her a wry smile. "I guess I better get back to him."

"I'll walk with you."

They entered the room to find Ryan still lying on the lounger. Dylan was there as well. He did a double take when he saw her walk in behind Ryan's mother. His brows rose.

"Ryan is ready to go for today. He did well. We were able to put the medicine in faster than we'd anticipated."

Ryan sat up. "I'll see you next week, Doc."

Dylan grinned. "I'll be here. Take care of yourself this week and be careful."

"Yes, sir."

Mother and son went out the door leaving the two doctors alone. Dylan said, "You and Ryan's mama looked pretty friendly there."

"We just ran into each other and had a little talk."

His mouth quirked up on one side. "Anything you want to share?"

"No, but she did give me some food for thought."

A nurse stuck her head in the doorway. "Dr. Nelson, you're needed out here a moment."

"I'll be right there." He glanced at Marcy. "See you later."

That evening Marcy was walking out of Dylan's office as he entered. "I was planning to ask you to dinner tonight, but I have a patient coming in through Emergency. I won't be leaving anytime soon."

"Oh." She knew he could sense the disappointment in her voice.

"Maybe we can do it tomorrow night."

"I'll look forward to it."

His lips spread into a bright smile. "I'm going to count on it."

Her heart swelled. She might be leaving soon, but she'd enjoy this feeling for as long as she could.

It was late. Dylan only intended to stop by his office long enough to pick up a file and his schedule for the next day. The light was still on. It wasn't like Marcy to leave it that way. He entered to find her with her head on her laptop, sound asleep.

For once she looked relaxed. All those serious lines around her eyes and mouth had eased. He brushed the soft curtain of hair back from her cheek with his finger. "Marcy."

Her eyes opened. She groaned and sat back, murmuring, "I only meant to rest my eyes, not fall asleep. What time is it?"

"Almost eleven. Way past time for us both to go home. Give me a sec and I'll walk you to your car."

"I have some more numbers to look at for a report." She opened her laptop.

He gently closed it. "That can wait until tomorrow."

To his surprise, she pulled out the drawer, retrieved her purse and stood. "You're right."

He picked up what he needed off his desk. "I'm glad you're finally listening."

"If I was more awake I might have something to say about that but right now I'm not up for witty sparring."

Dylan chuckled as he hustled her out of the office and turned off the light. "Good to know. I'm not sure I'm sharp enough to keep up."

Marcy giggled. *Giggled.* It made his blood run hotter. She sounded happy, free. Putting his hand lightly at her waist, he walked her to her car.

The parking lot only had a few cars in it at that time of day. Marcy opened the driver's door and dropped her purse inside before she turned to him. "I forgot to ask, how did the emergency go?"

Dylan pushed a hand through his hair. "I had to admit him. The boy's breathing is shallow. I'm afraid it'll be time to send in hospice soon. I never like to admit defeat."

Marcy touched his cheek then let her hand fall. Dylan had the idea she wanted to say something but couldn't get it out. "We shouldn't have to."

She sounded so sad he couldn't help but fold her into his arms. He'd worked for days not to touch her, afraid he'd want more than she could return or was willing to give, but right now they both needed human contact. To feel the other's beating heart.

Marcy gripped his shirt as she pressed her face into his chest. They stood there holding each other, absorbing each other's strength.

When she looked up, it felt like an invitation and Dylan couldn't help but place his lips on hers. Marcy's hands pulled him tighter as his mouth moved against hers. She moaned. He pressed her against the car as he teased the line of her lips.

The lights and sound of the security cart drew his attention. He quickly backed away.

"Everything okay here?" an older heavyset man asked from the cart.

"Yes. Just a late night. I was seeing her to the car."

The security guy gave Dylan a knowing nod. "Good. It's not safe for a woman to be out by herself at this time of night. Have a good evening." He drove off.

Marcy had already settled in the car.

As much as he wanted to touch her again, he didn't. "I'll follow you. Make sure you get home safely." When she started to speak, he stopped her. "Please don't argue. It's for my peace of mind too."

Marcy had stayed up for the rest of the night thinking about Dylan kissing her. She didn't understand this new feeling of insecurity. Her nerves hummed at a mere thought of Dylan. What had started as a comforting action

turned to a meeting of emotions that went into overdrive. If the security man hadn't come around, she wasn't sure what might have happened in the parking lot. At least on her part.

She'd been on her own for so long. Even after Toby died and Josh wasn't around much, she hadn't had this need to see and talk to him. Dylan had gotten past her wall. She was still confident she couldn't trust herself not to let him down, but she badly wanted his touch.

The minute Toby had died, her marriage had as well. Josh accused her of letting it happen. That she'd been so focused on her fellowship she'd not paid enough attention to her child. He played the blame game. She listened. More than that, she'd started to believe it even before Josh accused her.

When she entered Dylan's office the next morning to finish what she started the night before she was shocked to find him sitting behind his desk, his head in his hands. "You look awful," she said.

His eyes were red rimmed. "Thanks. That's what every guy wants to hear."

"Sorry, that wasn't a very warm greeting, was it?" Marcy stepped down the hall, returning with a cup of hot black coffee. She set it in front of Dylan. Her heart went out to him, and she asked gently, "How's your patient?"

"Not very good."

"I'm sorry to hear that."

"I am too. Steve and his parents have been through the mill. He was in remission for four years and now the leukemia has returned."

"That's awful." She couldn't make herself leave his side, but she didn't dare touch him. Toby hadn't even had the remission time.

"Yeah, I've tried everything I know to do," Dylan said, sounding defeated. Something she'd not heard before.

Her chest tightened and she asked quietly, "Would you mind if I look at his chart?"

Dylan picked up his electronic pad and touched the screen entering a few numbers, then handed it to her. "I welcome any ideas."

She sat down behind her desk to read the boy's chart. "What kind of health is he in currently?"

"Good actually. He's started running a fever and throwing up recently. But otherwise, he's regained his weight and all his vitals are good except for his white blood count, of course."

"Then he sounds like a good candidate for what I have in mind."

Dylan looked over his desk. "And that is?"

She met his gaze. "I want to put him in my trial. Try TM13. But in bolus amounts. Stop what's going on before it starts."

"But he doesn't fit the criteria or the trial parameters." Dylan came to stand beside her desk.

"No, but I believe by the numbers and the responses I've been getting that it could help."

Dylan gave her an intense look. "We could get in trouble stepping out of protocol. Maybe even lose our medical licenses."

"We could save his life," she snapped. "I'm willing to take the chance and the flak. His case is tailor-made for what I've been working on."

Dylan didn't say anything for a moment then nodded. "I am too. Let's go see if he and his parents agree."

"Do you think they will?" She started out the door.

"I think the parents are desperate and will agree to anything. I know I would."

"I would." She would have.

"Will you explain how the medicine works and answer questions?" Dylan pushed the button to the elevator.

"Certainly."

Once again, she and Dylan were partners. They made a good team. She'd never felt like she was a real partner with Josh. With Dylan they were equals. For once since Toby's death, the guilt was pushed away to focus on the task. Because Dylan believed in her.

Dylan had been excited and relieved to see Marcy walk through the office door that morning.

The night before he couldn't help reliving their kiss. He'd promised himself he wouldn't overthink it or read more into it than there might have been. Yet, he yearned to pull her into his arms again.

Between being worried about his latest patient and the emotional upheaval with Marcy, the morning had been long and difficult. And his father had called again. Nope this wouldn't be a good day.

Even as exhausted as he was last night it had taken him hours to go to sleep. He couldn't stop thinking about Marcy. Especially her reaction to his kiss.

He'd installed her in his office, his professional life and his personal life, making him miserable and happy at the same time. Something had to give. She would be leaving in a

couple weeks. His life would return to normal. Would his life be better for it? Or worse?

At least with his patient he and Marcy had a chance to help him. They'd found common cause. He liked working with her. She was efficient, intelligent, determined and compassionate. All qualities of a first-rate doctor.

Dylan knocked, then entered a room on the fifth floor. Inside sitting in a chair was Steve, a fourteen-year-old boy who should have been out playing basketball. Instead, he was stuck in the hospital. Sitting near him were his parents. Steve had grown over the years to the point he was almost too long for the bed. He'd been one of Dylan's first patients after he'd joined the staff of Atlanta Children's. If Dylan didn't known better, he would never say the boy was ill.

"Steve, Mr. and Mrs. Tiffon…this is Dr. Montgomery. She's a cancer research doctor. She's doing a trial here at the hospital right now." Dylan looked at Steve. "Do you know what a trial is?"

Steve shook his head.

"It means we give you an experimental medicine we have tested in the lab and now we're testing on a certain group of patients before we give it to everyone. There may be side effects for some. Dr. Montgomery believes this new medicine she has developed could help you. We'd like to try it on you. But we all need to agree."

Mr. and Mrs. Tiffon came to stand beside the bed. "Dr. Montgomery, why don't you explain to Steve and his parents about how the medicine works?"

"The drug is called TM13. It works on the T cells which are part of your immune system. I'm sure you've heard of those before."

The parents nodded and Steve looked bored.

"These T cells are part of our blood that fight off infection. Fight off cancer."

"We'll give you an intravenous dose starting now if you agree. Then another one or two, tomorrow and the next day. Then you'll have to come back once a week for a month. We'll be checking your blood work regularly."

"That doesn't sound much different than what it was when I was taking chemo," Steve muttered and took a moment to look at Dylan.

He nodded. "It's close to the same regimen but the medicine is different. It's new and we can't promise what side effects you might experience. The medicine hasn't been given to many people. Only tested in the lab. It may not work but we have high hopes that it will.

"What we do know is that what we've been doing isn't working." Dylan picked up the electric pad and made a note on it. "Dr. Montgomery and I are going to step outside and let you discuss this and think about it carefully."

He followed Marcy out into the hallway. They stood to one side.

"Do you think you'd agree with us if you were in their situation?" Dylan asked with concern filling his eyes.

"I would agree to anything for a chance to save my child's life."

CHAPTER SIX

"DID YOU THINK you would be this involved with the patients when you decided to oversee the trial?" Dylan leaned against the wall across the hall from Steve's room.

Marcy pursed her lips. "Actually, it hasn't been too bad. I've learned a lot. Ryan's mother made me think about things I hadn't before. And with Steve, I think I have a way to help him. If he and his parents agree."

"By the way, what does TM13 stand for? Or is it just a name pulled out of the air?"

"It's named for a patient, and it was the thirteenth time the medicine was reworked before we found the dosage that was right."

Dylan shifted. "I always hate waiting."

Marcy gave him a look of disbelief. "Isn't that more than half of what medicine is about?"

"Yeah. But I don't have to like it. I waited

so much when Beau was sick I never wanted to do it again, but then I went into a profession that waits all the time. Waits on blood work…waits for a few days to see what's going to happen. Waits until the test results are in. I still don't like it."

"Beau?"

"My roommate in boarding school."

"Oh, the friend who made you get into oncology. Will you tell me about him?" Marcy asked softly.

Dylan took a deep breath. For some reason he wanted her to know. To understand what had formed him. "Beau was my rock, my stability during a lonely time in my life. I was homeschooled for many years. Then my parents were reassigned to an area where I couldn't go to the local high school so it was decided that we, my older brother and I, would go to boarding school. Beau was my roommate and best friend. We were inseparable until Beau was ill one morning. He went to the infirmary and never returned. No one would tell me what happened. Finally Beau's mother called to tell me he had cancer and was in the hospital. I had no car and no way of visiting. All I could do was call and check on him. When I did talk to him, he sounded so depressed. That's when I decided to be a doctor and vowed to not do everything Beau's doctors did, except for making him well."

Steve's mother stepped into the hall and looked around until she spotted them and waved them inside. Marcy glanced at Dylan then led the way into Steve's room.

They were all standing around Steve's bed when he said, "I want to try it."

Dylan was positioned at the foot of the bed. "I believe you're doing the right thing."

Steve's mother, her face drawn with worry, said, "We have to try anything that might help him get better again."

"Then I'll start getting all the paperwork together. It'll take us a little while, but I'll get on it right away." Marcy gave them a reassuring smile. "I'll have to get permission to give it in a bolus fashion. As soon as I have that we'll move ahead."

Dylan, with Marcy shadowing him, headed toward his office. "I have to speak to the committee leader dealing with trials and write this up as a proposal. Get an emergency agreement."

"Today?"

"That's my plan."

"I need to decide how to incorporate this

into the trial. As it is, it won't be looked on favorably," Marcy said, her expression showing determination.

Dylan nodded. "That will help my chances of getting the okay. If he's under your trial guidelines than he'll fall under your proposals and not so much the hospital's."

"I'll write it up as a latecomer to the trail."

"Steve and his parents deserve this chance. Let's dot our 'i's and cross our 't's." Dylan looked at Marcy, hoping she would see that he shared her resolve.

"I hope that TM13 performs as I expect. That I haven't oversold it."

Marcy left to go to the clinic and organize the medicine.

By the time he'd finished what he needed to do she'd joined him again in the office. "I've ordered the medicine for Steve. I want to be there when the infusion is started."

Six hours later, when they entered Steve's room, a nurse was there, checking his vital signs. Another nurse joined them carrying a clear IV bag of TM13. She hooked it to the pole on wheels near Steve's bed. Marcy stayed out of the way as the nurse went about putting an IV in Steve's arm and securing it with tape.

Steve didn't even flinch as the nurse did what was necessary. He'd had so much experience with being in the hospital. He was a handsome youth with red hair and light blue eyes. He spoke with intelligence to Dylan about sports, baseball in particular.

Despite the conversation Dylan could tell he was keenly aware of what the nurse was doing. There were worry lines across his forehead.

Dylan could see that Marcy was watching carefully. He was positive that she hadn't given them all false hope, and prayed she was equally confident of that. She knew her facts and figures as one of the top researchers in her field.

Soon the precious clear liquid ran into Steve's vein, giving him a chance to kick out the invader. All that could be done now was to wait. The very word and action Dylan hated but was necessary.

Lab work would be taken regularly to try to catch any adverse effects, starting three hours after the dose had finished and continuing throughout the night They wouldn't know if they were making any real headway until after a few draws.

Dylan stepped out of the room and indicated for Marcy to come with him. They crossed the hall to a consult room. "I'm gonna stay around up here a little longer to see that everything's going well. You feel free to go back to the office. I'll call if something comes up."

"Okay. Can you see that lab results are forwarded to me? I want to review the findings. I'll be in the office if you need me."

Dylan checked his wristwatch. "The first blood draw won't be until 4 a.m. We won't know anything until then."

"This is our case. I'll be staying close," Marcy stated firmly. Dylan didn't argue with her any further. He was grateful to have her there. She knew all the ins and outs of TM13, had seen its reactions. He believed in Marcy's abilities as a doctor. Trusted her as a human being and admired her as a person.

Marcy sat behind her desk and checked her clock. It was still awhile before Steve's blood work would be drawn. Her phone rang. She picked it up and read one o'clock on the screen.

"Steve is throwing up." Dylan's voice held a desperate note.

She stood. "I'm on my way."

Headed to Steve's room, she stopped by the nurses' station to put on a mask and plastic gloves. She knocked then entered the room. Dylan along with the parents stood whispering in the corner, and Steve appeared to be asleep.

Dylan stepped to her.

"This isn't unexpected," she assured him. "We can handle it." Their roles had been reversed: she was now the one reassuring him. "I've seen this before. When the rate is slowed Steve should improve."

"I'll take care of that right away." Dylan stepped away to talk to the nurse who had just come in. From the look on Dylan's face, he was completely invested in Steve.

"His blood pressure and heart rate are up." The concern in Dylan's voice tightened her chest.

Marcy examined Steve's nailbeds. They had turned a dusky blue.

"He's also developed a rash on his abdomen."

Marcy checked the monitors. "You should also increase the rate of fluids."

Steve's eyelids opened.

"How're you feeling?" Dylan asked the boy.

"Not too good."

Marcy stepped to the bed. "Can you tell me what's bothering you?"

"My stomach. It's rolling." Steve wore a pained look on his face.

Marcy couldn't help but feel sorry for the boy.

Steve put his arms across his midsection and groaned.

"Nurse, could we please get some Phenergan in here," Dylan snapped, using a tone Marcy hadn't heard from him.

The young nurse hurried out of the room.

"I would also like to see a full blood panel," Marcy whispered to Dylan as she pulled a chair up beside Steve's bed later that evening.

Dylan brought his chair up next to hers. From their vantage point they were out of the way of the nurses but could see the monitor and Steve's face clearly.

She reviewed the numbers again on the digital pad then settled in the chair. She'd become concerned about Steve despite her confidence in her plan. With the additions of other medicines Steve's heart rate was coming down and BP was improving. The infusion of TM13 had been slowed but as much medicine as possible as soon as possible was the overall answer.

"Where are Steve's parents?"

Dylan settled in a chair. "I sent them home for some rest. I told them I would call them. I assured them I'd be here the entire time."

"They trust you, don't they?"

"I sure hope so."

"You're a special doctor and man, Dylan."

He gave her a thin-lipped smile as he watched Steve. "I like hearing you say so."

Hours later Marcy shifted in the metal chair with a thin cushion and narrow armrests. None of which made for a comfortable rest.

"You can sure tell these are institutional seating." Dylan yawned and stretched out his long legs, crossing them at the ankles.

"I think hospitals buy them to encourage visitors not to stay too long." She chuckled quietly.

"Why don't you get some rest? Put your head on my shoulder. I'll take the shift watching."

Marcy wasn't sure she wanted the nurses to think there was something going on between her and Dylan. She wasn't confident there was, yet that hot kiss in the parking lot said they both felt something more than friendship. Since she'd renewed her friendship with Dylan she'd started to live again. She could feel it. For too long she'd just existed. He'd filled the hole in her life with excitement and happiness.

She rested her head against Dylan's shoulder. Before she knew it, her eyelids drooped.

Dylan jostled her. She'd only been asleep for thirty minutes. "They're taking blood work right now. We should have the results back soon. I thought you'd want to see them."

Marcy groaned and uncurled, rolling her shoulders. "What I wouldn't give for a soft bed."

His gaze met hers. "Me too." Offering his hand to help her up. "Let's get a cup of coffee while we wait. Steve seems to be resting comfortably right now. The nurse is okay with checking in on him more often while we're gone. I suspect in a couple more hours his mom and dad will be here."

She and Dylan found fresh coffee in a little break room behind the nurses' station. They took a seat at a small table for four in the tiny space.

"It's been a long time since I've done an all-nighter," Marcy said.

Dylan sipped from his cup. "I don't do them often."

She studied Dylan a moment. "Steve is a special case."

"Yeah, he is. My first success case. He reminds me of Beau. Tough but easygoing."

"I think I'd like Beau. I'd like to meet him."

"You will. His family lives in Birmingham. He and Lisa will be coming for the ball. His company underwrites the event's expenses, which means all the funds raised go directly to help the children. They always make a huge donation each year."

"I look forward to it. I'll be leaving the day after the ball." Her chest tightened at the idea.

A nurse came to the doorway. "Dr. Nelson, the results are back. You can see them at the nurses' station."

They followed her to a computer, where she punched in a code and data filled the screen.

"His numbers have improved," Marcy said. "But just marginally. We've got to get them down further."

Dylan put an arm around her shoulders and squeezed. "It's going the right direction because of your recommendations."

Marcy glowed under his praise. "I don't think I can take all the credit."

"I think you should get a huge chunk of it."

"Now that we know Steve is headed in the right direction why don't you go on home and get some rest?" Dylan started out of the nurses' station. "I'll watch over Steve during the second dose."

"Why don't we both go when Steve's parents get here?"

Dylan shook his head. "Think I'll hang around awhile and see how he does. This is paperwork day anyway."

Marcy laughed. "You're using paperwork as an excuse to keep an eye on a patient."

"Yeah, I am. He's still not out of the woods yet. We have to hope the treatment works."

She squeezed his arm. "I truly believe it will."

He looked her in the eyes. "I appreciate you being here."

Marcy liked the idea that Dylan needed her and that she was able to help.

They reentered Steve's room to find him awake.

"Hey, buddy, how are you feeling?" Dylan stepped to the bed.

"Better."

Dylan looked at the monitors. "That's good

to hear. Your blood work came back with improvements this morning."

"You stayed all night?" Disbelief hung in the boy's question.

"Yep. Did you know you snore?" Dylan pulled his stethoscope from around his neck.

Steve's smile was weak, but it was a smile.

The door opened and in came his parents. They looked relieved to see their son sitting up in the bed. Dylan explained what had happened through the night and the plan for the next few days.

Minutes later Marcy stepped out in the hall behind Dylan with a sense of relief and success. She'd seen a positive sign in her life's work. What she had worked most of her adult life to achieve. It felt good but she wanted more. For once the guilt had eased.

"I'm going to stay here through the next dose." She glanced at the tech pad. "I want to see these numbers look better. I'm not satisfied. I have plenty of work I can do while I wait."

Dylan glanced at Marcy working at her desk. He'd thought it wouldn't be an issue to share his office with her, but it was turning into a real problem. He had welcomed her into his professional life and she was nudging her way into his personal life too. He was confused by his mixed emotions about her and the upheaval he felt at the change in him. He couldn't continue this way.

She would be leaving very soon. All he had to do was survive until then. Keep his hands and his lips to himself. Then his life would return to normal. Even now, looking exhausted, she pulled at him, making him want to take her into his arms.

Unable to continue being in the room with Marcy without going to her, he decided to leave her alone. He went to the Infusion Room to check on the patients there. A couple of them had questions about the ball but most were planning to attend.

"Have ya'll picked out the rap you're going to do?" He received several nods. "Anyone want to share with me?"

They all grinned and shook their heads.

An hour later he visited Steve's room. Inside, sitting beside Steve was Marcy. She was quietly talking to the boy's parents. After sleeping in a chair all night and working part of the day, Marcy still looked lovely.

It wasn't until Steve said, "Hey, Doc," that Dylan looked away.

"Hi. How're you feeling?"

"Pretty good. My stomach isn't hurting anymore." Steve put his hand on his middle.

"That's good to hear but that might not last for long. You're due for your next treatment."

The boy's face drew serious. "You think I'll be sick again."

Dylan turned as Marcy joined him beside the bed. "Maybe it won't be so bad this time."

"I hope so. It wasn't much fun last night." Steve fiddled with the edge of his blanket.

"I'm sure it wasn't," Marcy said, patting his arm. "We'll do our best to head it off this next time."

A nurse entered carrying the bag of liquid. She hung it on the pole before preparing the IV to hook it to Steve.

"We'll be here or close by all the time. All you have to do is ask for us," Marcy told him.

"Yeah, buddy, just let us know what you need."

Steve nodded then looked at the IV leading into his arm.

Marcy and Dylan stepped out the door.

"How do you think he's going to do?" Dylan asked looking back at the room with concern. He hated to put the boy through more but knew it was necessary.

"To be truthful I don't know. TM13 is strong with fewer side effects but given as a bolus dose I can't promise what might happen. That's why I'm going to stay close by. I not only need to see the results but the reactions. Plus I want to be here for them all."

"I understand how you feel so I won't try to get you to go home. But what I will do is show you where you can shower, find clean clothes and get some rest."

"That sounds nice, but I want to hang around here until still infusion is finished and I can check Steve's numbers."

Dylan sighed. "I can't fault your dedication. I plan to hang around for a while as well. Thank goodness it was a slow patient day in the clinic."

"But we do have the kids who are planning to sing coming in for practice and a pizza party this afternoon." Marcy yawned.

Dylan shook his head. "It always amazes me that they're on chemo, which often causes an upset stomach, and yet they'll still go for pizza. The strength of the young is outstanding." He regarded Marcy's pale face and reiterated his offer. "We're a phone call away, so why don't I show you where you can get a shower."

Marcy fixed him with a look. "Are you trying to tell me that I smell?"

Dylan smiled. "No more than I do. We've been at this for almost forty-eight hours. I think we deserve a shower."

Dylan directed Marcy into a locker room. "With any luck I can find you a set of scrubs to change into." He went to a cabinet and pulled out a plastic-covered prepackaged set of light blue scrubs. He handed it to her. "These should work. Please be sure to return them because you'll be charged for them."

"Thanks. I will," she said, taking the package from him.

He searched through the stack and pulled out another set of scrubs. "While you're changing, I'll check on Steve."

Marcy gave him a long look.

"Is something wrong? What's that look for?" He watched her.

"Because you are you." She gave him a quick kiss on the cheek.

He grinned. "I need to know what I did so I can do it again."

"You believe in me. Trust me with Steve."

Dylan did, even when she didn't seem to have that much confidence in herself. Did she have people in her life who didn't believe in her?

"Of course I do. Why wouldn't I? You're smart, educated and tops in your field." What he wanted to say but didn't was that she was also beautiful. He smiled. "What's not to believe in?"

She blushed a little and smiled. "Thank you. That's one of the nicest things someone has ever said to me."

Six hours later they studied Steve's blood work numbers on the computer screen.

"His white count has dropped but not far enough," Dylan noted, pointing to a number. He wasn't telling Marcy anything she didn't know.

"Yes, but it isn't enough to warrant not doing the third dose tomorrow. Just follow the same procedures as last time and I believe he'll be fine. At least the nausea was better this time around."

"I'm going to trust your judgment on this." Dylan started toward Steve's room.

Marcy's heart swelled. He trusted her. He still found her reliable. Her husband had never been able to do that after Toby's death, even before he'd started doubting her.

Dylan turned when she didn't follow. "Is something wrong?"

She smiled. "No everything is right." It wasn't until that moment she'd realized how much she needed someone to believe in her. Having Dylan's loyalty made her have faith in herself.

After the pizza party in a conference room with the patients singing at the ball, she and Dylan returned to their office.

"That went well. I think the kids are looking forward to performing now. At first I wasn't so sure. Wasn't even sure they'd show up." Marcy sank into her chair.

"Yeah, I believe they will be a hard act to follow. Marcy, I wish you'd go home. Get some sleep in a real bed, not a cot in a closet."

She gave him a defiant look and asked, "Are *you* going?"

He met her gaze. "Well, no."

"Then I think I should stay. The final dose can be given at 4 a.m., and I want to be here for it." Marcy squared her shoulders.

"But you have plenty of time to go home and come back." His tone was a plea.

"So do you," she countered.

"Okay. If we aren't going home, then at least we're going to get outside for a few minutes before the sun sets. I also think Steve and his parents could use a few minutes when we aren't hovering." He took her hand and tugged her toward the door.

She looked around. "Where're we going?"

"For a walk. There's a park just a couple of blocks from here." Dylan clicked off the lights.

"I don't think—" She stopped.

He took her elbow and nudged her forward. "Doctor's orders."

They headed out the staff door. Dylan directed her along the sidewalk and across the street then entered a gated path. Dylan led her along an easy trail to a creek. The birds chirped and flew away while the squirrels played in the trees. She watched in amazement when Dylan grabbed her arm, putting his finger over his lips in the sign for silence. He pointed to a rabbit.

"I must admit this is wonderful. I might not have thought I needed it, but I did." She smiled and rolled her shoulders.

"Sit. Let me massage your shoulders. Those hospital chairs aren't made for sitting in a long time or sleeping." She sat on a smooth rock and Dylan positioned himself behind her.

"You can't be much better off." He gave her a look filled with concern.

"Then we'll take turns." He placed his hands on her shoulders and started working the tight muscles there.

"That feels so good." A few minutes later she pulled away. "Your turn now."

Dylan sat next to her and presented his broad shoulders.

"No argument?" she teased.

"Are you kidding? I'd never turn a shoulder rub down. I hope I don't embarrass myself by purring."

Marcy chuckled. She placed her hands on him, kneaded his muscles while enjoying touching him but reminding herself she shouldn't let it go beyond this. "I feel guilty about being out here in all this beauty and tranquility while Steve is going through what he is."

"He was feeling fine when we left. I gave strict instructions if that changed to call me. I hate it too, but the procedure had to be done. Guilt does no one any good."

Marcy knew that too well. "You really believe that, don't you?"

"I do. For years I felt guilty about my parents missing every major event in my life. I thought it was my fault."

She moved so she could look him in the eyes. "It wasn't. I'm sure they didn't realize how much it bothered you. Did you ever tell them?"

He shrugged. "No."

She couldn't hide her sympathy. "It still must have hurt."

"You're right about that. I just know that I won't treat my children that way." Dylan pulled a package of crackers out of his pocket. "Not much of a picnic but what I could come up with on short notice."

Marcy noticed the abrupt end to the conversation but didn't comment. They ate sitting on the rock in the last sun of the day. Dylan took her hand, gently rubbing a thumb across the top, creating a calm within her she wouldn't have thought possible.

"Thanks for bringing me out here. You were right. I needed this. It gets your head away from your worries."

Marcy shivered. Dylan pulled her close and wrapped an arm across her shoulders. "We'll stay only a few minutes longer."

Unable to help herself, she leaned her head against his chest. The fleeting thought that she'd like to stay there forever entered her mind. She pushed it away. That would never happen. She wouldn't let it. Instead of wishing for something she couldn't have, she concentrated on the water flowing over the stones in the creek.

When Dylan finally moved, she sat straighter. He stood, offered his hand and pulled her to him. Their gazes met, held. His head lowered a fraction as if he thought to kiss her before he said, "We better get back. We have a patient waiting."

He held her hand as they strolled back the way they came. They walked in silence until Dylan broke it. "What do you see yourself doing ten years from now?"

She stopped and leaned back so she could see his face. "Wow, that's an out-of-the-blue, deep question. Are you asking about my work or my personal life?"

"Both. I'd like to hear your answer." His tone implied he wouldn't let her get away with not answering. Yet she would try. "How about you go first."

Dylan didn't even have to think. "I see myself here in Atlanta working at the hospital doing what I am doing right now, saving all the children I can. Hopefully with a wife and family."

Marcy could see too well a swing set in his backyard with children playing. Him coming home from a long day and them running to welcome him. What she didn't want to see was the woman walking toward him with a smile on her face. A sick feeling clenched her stomach. The face wasn't hers. Nor the mini-van in the driveway.

"Now you." Dylan said when it took her so long to respond.

She bit her bottom lip. At one time she had dreamed. But not now.

Dylan ran a gentle finger across her mouth, easing her hold, sending a shiver of desire through her.

"I want to find a cure for this horrible disease that ruins children's and families' lives."

He encouraged her to walk on. "That's admirable but don't you want something for yourself?"

Why did he have to keep pushing? That *would* be for herself. "That's what I've been working toward for the last ten years." Since Toby had died.

"No other dreams?"

"I think the one I have is large enough."

CHAPTER SEVEN

DYLAN CHECKED AND double-checked Steve's monitor and last lab work at 7 a.m. as he stood at the end of his patient's bed. The numbers were almost perfect. He looked at Marcy next to him. She glowed with pride.

Dylan's attention returned to his patient. "Your numbers look better. I'm cautiously optimistic that the drug therapy worked. You're going to have to stay here a few more days to make sure but I can see you going home."

A soft sob came from the direction of Steve's mother, who clung to his father's arm.

Dylan smiled. "I think we could all use some rest. The nurses will be keeping a watch over you. Dr. Montgomery and I are going to leave you to rest now. We'll see you tomorrow."

Steve nodded. His mother gave him and

Marcy a hug. The father shook their hands, stammering, "Thank you. Thank you."

Dylan noticed Marcy's eyes glistened as he closed the door to the room behind them. He couldn't help but burst into a grin. His arms came around Marcy, bringing her into a tight hug. "Apparently the fourth time is the charm."

"It worked," Marcy said in a breathy voice as she hugged him back.

Dylan let her go just as abruptly as he'd taken her, scared to reveal his true emotions, then put some space between them. "Yes, it did," he said. "Thanks to you, Steve has another chance. Now it's time we go home and get some real sleep. I'm exhausted and I know you must be too."

To Dylan's amazement Marcy offered him no argument. In the parking lot, Dylan said, "I arranged for Security to drive us home. Neither of us needs to be driving. We are exhausted."

Again, Marcy said nothing and just got in the car. She lay back in the seat and closed her eyes.

The sound of jackhammers and equipment surrounded Marcy's apartment when they pulled into the complex. A busted water main was being repaired.

Dylan's mouth tightened. "You can't stay here. You'll never get any sleep or a shower You can stay in my guest room."

"I don't think—"

"Be reasonable, Marcy." He waved a hand in the direction of the work. "This is a loud mess."

She looked around in defeat. "Okay, thank you. For tonight only, though."

A long roll of thunder and a loud boom woke Dylan just before midnight. He'd left the French door in his living area open letting in fresh air. Padding into the room that had grown thick and humid, he went to the wind-blown door. A storm was coming.

A movement grabbed his attention. Marcy.

She stood on the terracotta pavers with her head back and face up to the sky. As he stepped out the door, she continued to stand there as if she had no idea it would rain soon. Lightning flashed and somewhere farther off thunder shook the air.

"Marcy what are you doing out here?"

She wrapped her arms around her waist as

she shook. "I had a bad dream. He died on a night like this."

Dylan's chest tightened. Was she sleep-walking? "Who died?"

"Toby."

He waited. She must be overtired. Unable to help himself he asked, "Toby?"

"My son."

Dylan sucked in a breath. Did she know what she was saying? Had she lost a son?

"It was storming that night too." She didn't move, just spoke as if a long way away.

"A car accident?" He wanted to go to Marcy but feared startling her.

Marcy shook her head slowly. "No. From cancer."

Dylan gasped. Some of her actions and re-actions made sense now. "I'm sorry. I didn't know."

"Because I didn't want you to. That I couldn't save my own child while I was try-ing to save your patients. You wouldn't have trusted me."

Dylan was shocked she might think that, but it didn't matter now. He made his voice low and soothing and stepped closer. Another flash of lightning went across the sky. "Let's go inside, Marcy."

When she didn't move, Dylan stepped behind her. He just wanted her to feel his reassuring warmth. With deliberate movement he drew her to him. Her head fell back against his shoulder. He slowly rubbed her arm.

He kissed the top of her head. "I think there's more to the story. You can tell me. I'm a good listener. It won't go any further than me. But let's go inside."

He'd wondered about some of her actions, but she never let on how hard it must have been for her to see patients. The past had to have come back in waves. No wonder she could empathize with the parents. She'd been one of them. Knew what they felt.

"He would be ten now if he had lived. He didn't make it out of infancy."

Dylan stayed still, waited.

Her voice was dull with remembered pain. "I was so absorbed in my work trying to prevent cancer I didn't see that Toby had it. Ironic, isn't it? A cancer researcher having a child with cancer and not seeing it. It had been there growing and growing and I had no idea. I didn't recognize it." A soft sob bubbled out of her throat.

Dylan's arms tightened around her, holding her steady. Marcy didn't resist. He wanted her to know he was there to support her. He held her close, saying nothing. His ex-fiancée always complained he could only give support to his patients. That he didn't let anyone else get close enough for him to really care about them on a personal level. He cared about Marcy. Deeply. He wanted to take the pain from her.

"The storm woke me, and the memories swamped me. It doesn't happen all the time but tonight they got to me."

"Probably because of the emotional roller coaster you've been on the last three days."

A short while later, after she'd relaxed, Dylan asked softly, "Will you tell me about Toby?"

As a rule, she didn't talk about Toby to anyone. Ever. It was too difficult. For days afterward she'd relive the happy days, the sad days and the horrible moments. Still did. Let the guilt slowly eat her up. But she couldn't tell Dylan that; couldn't admit that to anyone.

They'd think she was crazy, not handling her grief. People had told her again and again that time would ease the pain. It didn't. She felt it as intensely as she ever had. The pain lingered like a bad smell. She could recognize it instantly. Yet for some reason she wanted Dylan to know. He had a way of making things better.

"By all standards Toby was a normal baby boy. When he started crying more than usual, we just thought it was a touch of croup."

"That's not uncommon."

"It is but that wasn't the problem. By this time, Josh had moved up in his firm and had to travel to sites more often. I got the majority of the care, but I was okay with that. We had great day care help as well, and an older lady came to the house. When Toby made a whistling sound as he breathed I took him to the pediatrician. He found a tumor in Toby's nose. He sent us to a pediatric oncologist. Toby was diagnosed with esthesioneuroblastoma."

"That's rare in a child." Dylan's voice said he was in doctor mode. She'd heard that tone before.

"It is. By the time it was diagnosed it was stage III." Her words came out low and measured. She had a difficult time saying them. "Less than a month later it had moved to a stage IV in the brain."

Dylan sucked in a shocked breath.

"I was a mess. Josh didn't handle it well

either. I felt—still feel—responsible for not recognizing the problem before I did. My ex blamed me. After all, I'm a doctor. I should've known. Seen it sooner."

"Marcy—"

She held up a hand. "I know what you're going to say. I've heard it all. But that doesn't change how I feel. Or the reality. The last few months of Toby's life were the worst. I took time off to be with him. Josh couldn't face what was happening and worked more not to think about it…then Toby was gone."

Dylan's arm tightened around her. She sank into his heat and comfort. Without saying a word he told her he was there for her.

She took a deep breath. "After Toby died, I threw myself into my work, which finished off my already rocky marriage. Here I am with something to really offer children with cancer, and I can't even tell the parents I see every day that I've been where they are."

Dylan continued to hold her. "But you've been helping them more than you know. I've seen you talking to Ryan's parents, Steve's and Lucy's. I even pointed out how you interact with them. The children and the parents all like you. I'm even more impressed now that I know about Toby."

She turned in his arms. "It just looks that way. Every day I have to remind myself to keep it together."

"Don't we all? I have to remind myself not to get too involved. Not to bring it all home with me."

"It just seems like the more progress we make with curing cancer the more children have it. It doesn't stop. I want it to stop." Her frustration tightened the muscles of her face.

He cupped her cheek, raising her face until she could see him clearly. "You and I are doing what we can to make that happen."

The moment warmed. His gaze held hers.

She needed the reassurance, the tenderness, the human interaction. It had been too long since someone had held her, desired her, comforted her. If she was honest with herself, she liked being with Dylan. Then why was she stopping herself from enjoying him while she could? It would be painful to leave him either way. She wanted the here and now. To grasp life for a change.

Instead of fighting her feelings she would accept them and share them with Dylan if he still wanted her. She pressed her lips to his.

Dylan's return kiss was gentle, caring and tentative. Soothing.

Her focus remained firmly on Dylan's tender, yet seductive lips. He pressed closer. It was a sweet reassuring kiss. Yet she wanted more. She needed someone to touch her, desire her. She leaned into him.

His mouth firmly found hers this time. His arms tightened around her as his lips pressed against hers. This wasn't a kiss of reassurance but of the want and need of a man. Her head spun. This was too much sensation. She hadn't been kissed since Josh left. Hadn't wanted that type of contact. She instinctively pushed against Dylan's chest.

His mouth immediately left hers. "I'm sorry. I shouldn't have done that."

She put some distance between them.

"You were upset. I just wanted you to feel better. I shouldn't have taken advantage of you." Yet he still wanted her in his arms again. Wanted to make that sadness he'd heard in her voice disappear.

"It's okay. I understand."

He'd forced himself to remain isolated from real emotional relationships, fearing that if he loved someone, they would leave him. After all, his parents had, Beau had no choice but to leave him, even Marcy had in her own fashion, then his fiancée. The lesson he'd learn long ago was he was destined to be alone.

Even with his parents the distance was not only in miles but emotions. They didn't know him, especially his father who couldn't understand that Dylan's place was in Atlanta not in some far-off country. He tried not to resent them, and he'd missed them desperately when he was a boy. That loneliness still colored his world. It was just as well Marcy wanted space. She would leave him soon too, for a second time.

"Let's get you inside. You're freezing. You need a warm shower before you start to shiver." Dylan led Marcy to the guest bath and turned the shower water to hot. "I'll get you something else to wear. Don't argue. Just get in."

She put a hand on his arm stopping him. Her wide sad eyes locked with his. "I'm afraid that my

life is passing me by. I have become nothing more than a lab rat. In a cage of my own making."

Dylan's chest constricted. Had he brought on this show of boldness by having her talk about the past? "You have more life to live. Plenty of love to give."

"Toby was so small and perfect. He didn't deserve to die that way." She sounded as if she were talking to herself instead of him.

"No, honey, he didn't. That's a part of life we can't do anything about."

"I can't seem to do anything about any of my life." She looked so sad, Dylan brought her against his chest. "I think you have more control than you believe. You've just been hiding and running away from your feelings. You haven't had the right person around to help you learn to live again."

She looked up with a luminous gaze. "Are you the right person?"

Dylan's chest tightened. What could he promise her? Nothing. He was self-reliant and had learned to appreciate his own company. Could he open up enough to let her in? Be the person she deserved. Dare he? Dylan took a moment to answer. "I'd like to think I could be."

Marcy couldn't remember the last time, if ever, she'd been so open with another person. Even Josh hadn't known all her fears and dreams. She wanted Dylan to see her as a desirable woman, not just a needy one. After the sad story she'd told he'd acted as if she were too fragile to touch. She'd pushed him away, but she needed his touch, wanted personal interaction. It had been so long since she'd dared to feel.

She'd held herself away from any intimate contact for so long she'd forgotten what it was like to have someone hold and kiss her. Or how her body trembled at a man's touch. Until she'd reconnected with Dylan any sexual emotions had been missing from her life. Right now, she felt too much. It was all jumbled together. Yet she knew she wanted Dylan.

Just the little bit of caring he'd given her by insisting she shower was more than she let herself experience in years. That had opened the door to need. She craved more as she stepped under the spray.

For too long she'd lived in fear, kept people at arm's length. If she didn't care, then she wouldn't get hurt. But with Dylan she was safe. He would never hurt her. She would leave soon. For once with good memories. She wanted to live for a change. At least for a little while.

Did Dylan want her? She had to be bold enough to ask.

"Dylan?"

"Yes?"

She opened the sliding glass door to the shower. "You must be cold too. Don't waste this hot water."

"Marcy?" Her name came out rusty and sexy. "Do you know what you're saying?"

"Uh, yes. I'm inviting you to share my shower."

"Marcy, do you know what you're doing to me?" His words had a strangled sound to them.

"I think so. I hope so. I want you. I want to feel alive again. To feel something. I want to sleep next to you."

Dylan wasted no time in stripping off his pajama pants. He was amazing in all his naked glory, and desire.

He stepped inside the shower and took her into his arms. "Are you sure about this? I don't want you to have any regrets in the morning."

She cupped his cheek. "The only thing I would regret is if I didn't kiss you."

"I can't deny I like that answer," he murmured, his lips finding hers with a tentative touch.

Marcy returned the kiss. She ran her hands

over Dylan's water-slick body, appreciating the dips and rises of his muscles. She intended to enjoy him for as long as possible.

His gentle touches turned urgent and the pressure of his fingertips encouraged her. His hands slipped over her body following her curves. Cupping her butt, he lifted her to him. She gripped his shoulders as his manhood stood strong and thick between them.

Marcy's hands wandered up his back and over his shoulders, encouraging him.

He wrapped her in his arms. His mouth left hers to travel across her cheek to her neck. He nipped at that tender spot behind her ear. Would she die from the pleasure? She moaned. Leaning her head to the side, she gave him better access. Her body trembled.

He kissed along her hairline to her temple as she stepped closer. His straining pulsing manhood stood hard against her middle. The fire of desire roared making her gasp.

The water cooled.

Dylan put some space between them. "I've wanted you too long to take you for the first time in a shower. You deserve better. You should be loved slow and easy, savored like a good wine."

She pressed her body tight against him and kissed him deeply.

Dylan leaned back where he could see her face. "Marcy, are you sure about this? There'll be no turning back if this continues."

Marcy went up on her toes and gave him a challenging kiss, opening her mouth in invitation. He accepted her offer and took over the kiss.

She ran her hands through his hair, along the back of his neck and across his shoulders. When he tugged at her bottom lip, she whimpered her gratification as if she'd never experienced anything so wonderful. She hadn't.

Marcy pulled away. Her gaze met Dylan's then roamed downward to his chest. She leaned forward to kiss him but thought better of it. Instead, she licked a rivulet of water running down the center of his torso. Dylan shuddered and Marcy smiled.

He nudged her away from him. "Marcy, we have to stop."

She straightened. Had she gone too far? Was Dylan disappointed in her? "Did I do something wrong?"

He groaned. "No, honey. The problem is you're doing everything too right."

Marcy smiled, her confidence restored.

"I want you more than I can say. Let's go to my bed. It's getting cold in here, anyway." He touched the tip of her hard nipple. "Even if I like what it does for your beautiful breasts."

She craved his touch, what it made her feel.

"I've wanted you since we were in college. I think I can wait ten minutes until I get you to bed."

Her face eased into relief. "You've wanted me that long?"

Dylan turned the water off and stepped out of the shower. "I think I've wanted you forever."

"You never said anything."

Taking her hand, he led her out of the shower before wrapping a towel around her shoulders. He rubbed her down, leaving her with the towel to use on her hair. "What was I going to say? *Give up your boyfriend for me? I didn't even have enough money to take you out on a real date.*" He pulled a towel off the rack and dried himself.

Marcy vigorously rubbed her hair. She peeked out from under the towel. "I'm more interested in you than a date."

The skin tightened across Dylan's cheekbones. "You're so beautiful."

Heat that had nothing to do with the steamy

shower warmed her. "Thank you. Age and a baby have changed me some."

"I like the mature you. You're more beautiful than you were in college. Leave the towel." Dylan tugged the material and it fell to the floor. He took her hand. "Come on, I'd like to show you just how beautiful I think you are."

The storm had settled in.

Dylan led her to his bed. Pulling back the covers, he let her crawl in and he joined her. He lay on his side and took her hand. Bringing it to his mouth he kissed her palm. "I need to know you're sure about this. I can't have you regretting this tomorrow. If you aren't sure, it stops here, and we go to sleep. I value our friendship too much."

No one had ever shown Marcy the sensitivity and attention Dylan bestowed. He understood her. Even Josh hadn't been able to make her feel this desire. The few men she'd made herself go out with since the end of her marriage hadn't come close to doing so. She wanted Dylan. Wanted this. Needed him.

She cupped Dylan's cheek. "I would never regret anything between us. You have my word we'll always remain friends. I need to live a little. Feel alive and I want to do that with you."

Closing the distance between them, he kissed her deeply. She wrapped her arm across his chest as she slid her leg between his legs. It felt so good to have human contact. To have someone tell her she was beautiful, to make her feel desired. To believe she had something to offer.

Dylan's hand traveled along the curve of her hip to her waist until it lifted her breast. His fingers kneaded gently, teasing her nipple, making it stand erect. He rasped, "So responsive."

His mouth left hers. He kissed the hollow of her shoulder before his lips circled her nipple and sucked.

Marcy's center tightened. She leaned back giving him free access as she ran her fingers through his hair, holding him close. Her breaths turned short and shallow. Could she die from such pleasure?

"Like that, do you?" Dylan asked as he moved to the other breast.

Marcy couldn't answer. All her attention was focused on how Dylan made her feel. She pulled at him, wanting to have him against her, but he resisted.

He raised his head, meeting her look. "Lie back and let me worship you. You deserve it."

She rested against the pillows. Her fingers fisted in the sheet. Dylan continued to love on her breasts. Lava-hot need flowed through her. His lips found the valley between her breasts. He kissed her there before moving on to her shoulders. Leaving them, he moved down one arm, sucked each of her fingertips then went to the other limb.

"You taste like honey and smell like my flower garden in the spring," he murmured against her skin as he kissed her waistline.

Using the tip of his tongue, he tormented her until she lifted her hips and yelped. His palms drifted over her behind. It was as if he was learning her many facets and memorizing them. Dylan gave her a thorough examination. "Perfect."

Slowly, too slowly, his hand floated over her stomach and moved lower. Marcy held her breath. Dylan's every touch, brief or languorous, made her sensitized skin sizzle. When his lips followed the path of his hands she sucked in her breath. She grasped his hair with both hands. Her body was wired tight. She bit her bottom lip in anticipation. Where would he explore next?

Dylan sat back reaching for one of her feet. He kissed the arch. Marcy shivered. This man was going to kill her. He raised her leg further, placing another kiss on the back of her knee. She squirmed.

Desperation washed through her. "Dylan! Please."

He grinned as he lightly ran his index finger over her calf, tickling the bottom of her foot before he stopped.

She tugged on her foot, but he kept it in a gentle but secure hold.

Dylan kissed his way up her leg. He didn't stop at her knee but continued along the inside of her thigh. She lifted her hips. His hand traveled along her other leg until he brushed the outside of her center.

"Oh... Oh!" Marcy breathed. If he didn't touch her soon, she might explode.

Dylan studied her a moment with desire burning in his eyes before his lips found hers. Seconds later his finger slid into her. She bucked. His tongue matched his movements.

Marcy shattered into the air and floated on bliss, until she came back together to settle with a deep sigh on the bed as a pile of boneless flesh.

Dylan's chuckle was one of male satisfaction. "That good, huh?"

Marcy ran her hand up his arm. It had been. Even better. One like no other. "Come here, I'd like to say thank you."

"I like the sound of that." His mouth found hers.

Wrapping her arms around him, she pulled him to her. She kissed him deeply. Dylan encouraged her to open her mouth and their tongues danced. She kneaded the muscles of his back as he continued to kiss her.

"I can't wait any longer to have you." He turned to the bedside table and jerked the drawer open. Removing a package, Dylan opened it and rolled the plastic covering over his impressive manhood.

He looked at her. She couldn't miss the admiration in his eyes. It was a look she'd never seen before but knew she'd treasure. She opened her arms. He came down beside her. Her lips joined his as he found his place between her legs. His hard length nudged her center. With a flex of his hips, Dylan entered her.

She tensed. It had been so long. Dylan pulled back and she raised her hips in invitation. He pushed forward, filling her. He looked into her eyes as he pulled back, then plunged again, picking up speed.

Hot need grew intense in her, tightened, then snapped. She spun off into that heaven only Dylan could create. As she returned to the real world, he pumped faster and deeper. His intent gaze bore into hers.

She had no doubt who was loving her.

With a final surge, he released a groan of pure satisfaction, shuddered before he lowered himself on his stomach beside her. His arm remained draped over her waist as if he didn't want to let her go.

The problem was she didn't know how she could stay.

CHAPTER EIGHT

DYLAN WANTED MORE of Marcy but they both needed rest. "We should get up. We have to be at work."

For once he wished that wasn't the case. If he had his way, they'd stay in bed all day. He'd lie with Marcy in his arms forever. But there were patients depending on him. And Marcy also had her work.

She lay half on his chest, snuggled against him. Her arm hung over one of his shoulders while a leg rested over his leg. He wanted her again. Not fast and frantic like his body demanded. Instead, slow and sweet like his heart desired. But it would wait.

She fit next to him perfectly. Too much so. When she had to leave part of him would go with her. This time would be worse than when he'd been in college.

He wanted to know all about her. There

was more to Marcy than she'd shared. He needed to understand her. "Will you tell me about your marriage?"

"You don't want to hear about that. I thought you said we needed to get moving."

He kissed the top of her head. "We have time. I want to hear. I think you need to talk."

"There's not that much to tell. After graduation I went off to Duke medical school the next fall. Josh found a job in town. His degree is in civil engineering, so he had no difficulty joining a good company. We married a year later. I finished up my third year and learned during residency that I was pregnant. It wasn't the best timing, but I was happy.

"By that time, I was gone for days sometimes, and he worked long hours. We didn't see much of each other. Having a baby added pressure to the marriage. Josh was happy but I was thrilled with the baby. I had already decided cancer research was the direction I wanted to go. I loved the idea of creating something that could save many lives and it also would give me steady hours, which would work with having a family. I had it all planned out."

"I bet you even had a list." His tone held humor, but his face remained somber.

She gave him a wry smile. "I did. Toby was born that spring. He was perfect. The best thing I've ever done. I fell in love instantly."

He felt the tremor go through her body. Had he asked too much of her?

"Things had started to get rocky between Josh and me. When Toby got really sick it didn't help the situation. Josh struggled with Toby being sick. We didn't always agree. He blamed me. He piled on the guilt that I already felt." She hadn't recognized all that then. "He wasn't a bad guy. He just didn't know how to handle his pain." She paused then continued, "For that matter neither did I. In the end he couldn't let go of blaming me. He couldn't forgive me for not seeing the problem sooner. I couldn't disagree with him."

Dylan squeezed her shoulder.

"Within a year we were divorced." She sat still a moment appreciating the movement of Dylan's hand across the tense muscles of her back.

"I know from working with cancer kids, it puts a strain on a marriage to have an ill child. The parents must be completely devoted to each other and think outside themselves to survive and hold the marriage together. It puts stress on any relationship. There's a 60 percent divorce rate for parents with a chronically ill child."

"There were already problems in the marriage before Toby. I realize that now..." Marcy's voice trailed off. "You know, I've talked about that time more with you than I have anyone." She sounded perplexed by the idea. "I have to admit it's been cathartic."

"I'm glad you think you can talk to me. I'm honored. I'm sure the last few cases we've seen together have been emotional for you. But you've been great and held it together," Dylan said. "I wish I had been there to help. I wish that hadn't happened to you. To Toby." He hugged her. Tight.

She held on to him. This was where she belonged now. In Dylan's arms.

"I'm sorry that happened. You deserve better."

She met his gaze. "Thanks for saying so."

He took a moment before he spoke. "I'm glad you told me. It helps me better understand you."

Marcy settled beside him again. "Josh was right. I should've seen the signs."

Dylan rolled to his side so he faced her

then said, "Being a doctor doesn't make you all-knowing."

"I was focused on my work. Doing all I could to get started in my career. I failed in that area."

His look bore into hers. "I don't believe that for a minute, but if you did, I'm sure it won't ever happen again."

She studied him. "I know it won't because I'm not going to have any more children. I'm not sure I'll ever remarry."

Dylan sat straighter. "I think that would be sad. Some child will miss out on having a wonderful mother. The world would miss out on a child you helped raise."

She gave him a weak smile. "That's a very nice thing to say."

He took both her hands and kissed her palms. "It's the truth. I'm not just saying it to make you feel better." Why did it matter to him so much that she believed him?

An hour later, after making love to her again he used his arm that lay along Marcy's back and across her waist to jostle her. "Hey, sleepyhead, we need to get ready for work."

"Want to stay here."

"Me too but Ryan is coming in for his

treatment today. We have Steve to check in on. Maybe to send home. His parents have worried enough—they don't need to be concerned about the doctors not showing up. Then we have to go by your apartment and get your stuff. I want you here with me."

She looked at him.

"Hey, why the frown?" he asked. Marcy shifted but he was slow to let her go.

She looked away and slid across the bed as far as possible.

"Marcy?"

Dylan's gut tightened. He could feel her pulling away. That wall of bricks she'd climbed over and knocked down last night was going up again. Sadly, he didn't know any way to stop her from running to the other side without making things worse. He needed time to think about his next move. If she'd even give him a chance to make one.

"Please don't do this."

"What? Try to maintain our friendship after a night of passion?" By her look of anxiety, he feared he'd gone too far.

"We need to get to the hospital. I don't wanna analyze it, conjugate or multiply what happened between us. Let's just accept that it was."

"'It was,' as in that was the only time?"

"You know it has to be."

"Why?"

She snatched a shirt lying on a chair and jerked it on. "Because I'm only here for a little while longer. I have all this baggage that I refuse to unload on you. Last night I said too much. You're a good guy but you don't deserve that. You need a woman who can give you a home and family. I can't be that person."

It had been his experience that men and women didn't go backward after sharing a night together, but if she wanted to try, he'd go along. "Okay. If that's the way you want it."

"Thank you for being such a gentleman."

"You can thank my parents for that."

Dumbfounded, Dylan watched Marcy hurry out the bedroom door. This wasn't what he expected for the morning after. Getting up and having a leisurely cup of coffee, holding hands across the table, yes. But Marcy going out the door without a backward look hadn't entered his mind. What had happened between their perfect lovemaking hours earlier and now?

If he was a lesser man, he might've felt

used. But he knew last night had meant more to Marcy than she let on. There was a real connection between them. In fact, there always had been.

Left in a bed going cold, he stepped into the shower, which brought back sweet memories of the night before. What would it take to remind Marcy of all those moments as well?

Marcy took care of necessities in the guest bathroom then splashed water on her face. Looking in the mirror she pushed her hair into some semblance of order. She noticed a new toothbrush and toothpaste along with a hairbrush sitting on the counter. Marcy stared at herself in the mirror. What type of man thinks about putting those out?

One with a big heart. Or one who thought of others first. Stayed prepared. She found the idea sweet. And far too much to her liking. Or did Dylan have women over regularly enough to always have items on hand. She didn't appreciate that idea.

Either way she gladly took advantage of them. She jerked on her well-worn clothes. Finished she went in search of Dylan. A noise in the kitchen let her know he was in there.

Dylan, dressed for the day in a collared shirt and slacks, stood at the stove. The table had been set. Two plates sat on the bar close to him. Bacon and toast were already on them. He stirred a frying pan of eggs. "Did you find everything you needed?"

"I did. Thanks for the toothbrush and the other stuff."

He watched her. "I want my guests to be comfortable."

"I found it interesting you keep those things around." She liked the guy he had become more and more but she couldn't let this go any further for his sake.

"Not that big a mystery. I'm a missionary's kid, remember. I keep the toiletries for my family when they come to visit. Not that they show up that often."

At least she could count on her family. She didn't care for that sad note in Dylan's voice. She nodded. "About a few minutes ago—"

"Hey, we're all good. Please don't ruin it by trying to explain it away."

She sighed. "You're really a nice guy. There are too few people I could ever say that about." She meant that. He was too fine for her.

He shrugged. "Let's just say I understand

what the important stuff in life is." He took a mug off a rack. "How do you like your coffee?"

She didn't want to answer but he deserved the truth. "I'm not really a coffee drinker."

"I think I've got a few teabags that Mom left here the last time they visited."

"Thanks, but I'd rather get to the hospital. I want to check on Steve."

"I've already called. He's doing great the nurse said. After we've had a civil moment over our morning drinks we'll go see for ourselves."

She shifted from one foot to the other. "I'd rather go now."

"Running, Marcy?" He scooped fluffy eggs onto the plates before moving around her to the table. Had he taken special pains not to touch her?

"No. Yes. Maybe. I don't know, Dylan. I need to think."

He took a seat at the table. "I get that. I could do some of that too."

Marcy gave him a weak smile. "I didn't plan—"

"Please just take a seat and eat your food."

Marcy's mouth clapped shut. She did as he asked.

* * *

Half an hour later a taxi dropped Dylan and Marcy off at the hospital front door.

He asked, "Are you going to be with me in the clinic today?"

"No, I've got some numbers to review especially related to Steve. I'll be in the office most of the day. I'll check patient charts this afternoon."

"Okay, then I'll see you later."

She didn't look at him as they parted in the stairwell, but before the door closed between them Marcy turned. "I'm sorry if you think I'm treating you badly. That's not my intention. I'm just not very good with moments like the one this morning. I need to think about what I want. Just give me a little space."

"You can have all the space you want. All I want is for you to be happy."

"Thanks, Dylan."

He thought he might be too nice. This professionalism wasn't what he envisioned happening between them this morning. Yet in many ways, like Marcy, he was trying to figure out what he wanted as well. He'd been a loner for so long, it scared him to think about how much last night had meant to him.

He had no doubt he wanted Marcy back in his bed.

His mind had gone to forever. Wow, that thought brought him to an abrupt halt in the hall. Could he really think long term? Did they even want the same things? He wasn't sure they did. She was running scared from her past. It had hurt him to hear her say she didn't ever want to have children again or marry. He wasn't sure why that disturbed him, but it did.

He'd had a taste of heaven and desired more. Just having Marcy in his arms took away the loneliness that had become so much a part of his life. With Marcy he felt freer, less burdened. Wanted. Until this morning.

Dylan started down the hall again. He needed to get up to see Steve then to his other patients. Still, Marcy's attitude worried him. She wasn't the only one standing in the rain, emotionally confused, hoping for an umbrella. The problem was he didn't know how to help her through whatever was eating at her. She seemed to lock everything away, stew on it. In his opinion she carried guilt that didn't belong to her.

The piece of their complicated relationship that rubbed him raw was that Marcy acted as if she had no intention of returning to his bed. That had been the last thing he expected to happen. Despite his disappointment in her attitude, his heart couldn't help but hurt for her.

She really had been through it. More than any person or parent should have to endure. She had been so happy-go-lucky when he'd known her in college. He'd seen flashes of that person in the last few weeks before she hid it away behind a seriousness she wore like armor. He wanted to strip off that covering and see it burned to never be worn again. Then Marcy would truly smile all the time, so that it showed in her eyes.

What he needed was a plan.

Over the next two days he treated Marcy like a colleague only. They saw patients in the Infusion Room and the general clinic. Lucy had come in for her treatment. Dylan had watched from across the room as Marcy spoke to the mother. Both the women needed the interaction and support. Marcy just wasn't as aware of that fact as Lucy's mother might have been.

Despite all the times he wanted to touch Marcy, he restrained himself. He gave her cheerful good mornings and smiles. To the best of his ability, he acted as if the night they had shared was nothing more than a pleasant memory. Yet the sexual tension between them remained thick. Gradually Marcy greeted him first, shared a smile. A couple of times she even initiated the conversation.

Late Thursday afternoon he stopped by the office to pick up some papers. Marcy was working at her desk. She glanced at him but returned to her work.

"Sorry to bother you but I thought you might like to know I spoke to Steve a few minutes ago and he's doing great." The boy had been discharged two days earlier.

"That's nice to hear." She had really gone back into her dark hole.

He needed to pull her out before she forgot what it was like to have human interaction again. Dylan started for the door, stopped. "Uh, you know I never got to take you out on a date. I'd like to. I'd planned for us to have pizza years ago. I can do better now. Would you like to have dinner with me tonight? I know you have work to complete but we can go when you get done."

"Dylan—"

"It's just a simple date. Nothing more. I won't even hold your hand if you don't want me to."

"I don't know."

"It's just a meal, Marcy. Share it with me." He had to remind himself not to lose his patience.

"Okay. I'll be ready to go at six."

He grinned. "I'll pick you up then."

"We could just leave from here. I could fellow you."

"Nope. I pick up my dates. See you at six." Dylan went out the door with a spring in his step.

Marcy slid out of Dylan's car as he held the door in front of the restaurant. His car suited the surrounding decor of the gleaming silver building. In one of the many large windows hung a red neon sign flashing the name Atlanta Café.

"Oh, 1950s, I love it." She glanced back at his car. "It suits your car."

He grinned. "Noticed that, did you?"

She chuckled. "Hard to miss."

Suddenly all the unease between them was gone. They'd found their footing again.

Marcy looked around and declared, "I like it."

"I'm glad to hear it." A warm light in Dylan's eyes made her middle tingle.

Inside the restaurant the tables were covered in white tablecloths with wooden chairs and a hurricane lamp sitting in the center. There was a simple elegance to the place.

"Hello, Dylan." A smiling older woman with an apron wrapped around her waist walked up to them.

"Marla. It's been too long." Dylan gave the woman a hug.

"I guess the hospital keeps you busy." She smiled at him.

"Unfortunately, it does."

"Let me show you to a table and get you fed." She settled them in a corner out of the way in the busy restaurant.

"I guess you come here often," Marcy said, looking around the dining area.

Dylan studied the menu. "Not that often."

"But they know you so well."

"That's because I took care of Marla's granddaughter." Dylan laid the menu down.

Marcy hesitated to ask but for some reason she had to know. "How's she doing now?"

"She's perfect. In college and already planning her wedding."

The tightness in Marcy's chest left. "That's wonderful."

He started to say something but stopped

himself before picking up the menu. "I was thinking pizza tonight, how about you?"

"I would like to share a pizza with you."

A waiter came to the table, preventing them from carrying the conversation further. Dylan ordered an extra-large pizza. When the waiter left, she looked at Dylan. "Are you sure that'll be enough?"

His dark eyes held a twinkle. "If it's not I'll order more. I feel like celebrating. Steve went home. Lucy's treatments are going well. Ryan looks to be improving and I think this will be the most successful Care Ball of them all. Thanks a lot to you."

"I don't think I did all that much." Still, it felt good to have Dylan's praise. "I hope you made it clear to Steve and his parents, as well as Lucy's, that TM13 isn't a cure. They still have a fight ahead." More than once she'd felt positive about Toby's recovery, only to have her hopes dashed.

"I agree but we've made a step in the right direction this past weekend. That's always worth celebrating, even if you don't have cancer. I was just thinking it's nice to celebrate life. It's too short to hold back."

Marcy didn't respond. She mulled over what Dylan was saying. He was right. Why hadn't she heard that before? Because she wouldn't allow herself to do so. Hadn't been open to the idea. Until Dylan. All those years she hadn't been living by that lesson, what had she failed to appreciate? Happiness?

She missed him the last few days more than she wished to admit. As good as her professional work had been going her life had felt off-center without him. She'd found joy with Dylan. Shouldn't she hold on to it as long as she could? At least while she had him.

He put his elbows on the table and clasped his hands. "Tell me what you're thinking over there."

Her gaze met his. "You're always asking me that."

"Because I'm always interested." His look didn't waver.

"I was thinking that you're right."

Dylan's brows rose almost to his hairline. "You think so? I didn't know you could be that positive."

"Have I really been that bad?" She didn't want to be like that anymore.

Dylan shrugged. "Pretty bad."

"That comes from working in a lab by myself much of the time. I've forgotten how to be social."

He touched her hand for a moment. "You need to get out more. You certainly haven't had any trouble being social with parents."

"Hanging out with you has made me do better."

"I sort of like the newer Marcy who's more like the older Marcy."

She laughed. "You don't even make sense. But thanks, I think."

The waiter returned with their pizza, and they started eating without saying much.

Marcy looked at Dylan. He really was an amazing person. One that she also admired for his intellect. She'd had enough of hiding her feelings. Of acting like there was nothing between them. She only had one more week in Atlanta, and she wanted to make the most of it—with Dylan.

He put down his fork. "What's that look about? Do I have something on my face?" He picked up his napkin and wiped his mouth.

"I was just thinking." She pushed her half-finished slice away.

His eyes narrowed. "Doing that again, are you? Okay give. What're you thinking?"

Dylan was being charming yet there was an undertone of insecurity in his voice. She didn't like it. He sounded distant as if they were strangers instead of a couple who had explored each other's bodies in detail just days ago. But hadn't she been the one who'd made it uncomfortable between them? Was this what she wanted? Her mouth tightened.

Dylan didn't play games. If anything, he was the most straightforward person she'd ever known. She didn't enjoy seeing that unsure look in his eyes or the cautious way he treated her. To make matters worse, her body craved his touch. Why shouldn't she have it?

Dylan continued to stare at her quizzically. "Now I'm really curious. Please tell me what you have on your mind."

"I'm ready to go home."

All the color left his face. "I'm sorry you aren't having a good time."

She picked up a sugar packet and fiddled with the corner before she looked directly at him. "I'm having a great time. I want to go home with you."

Dylan's eyes widened. Desire flickered in them, wild and bright. His gaze didn't leave hers. He stood and dropped two large bills on the table then offered her his hand. She slipped hers into his larger one. Within minutes they were in the car.

Dylan asked with a hard note in his voice,

"Are you sure about this? I want no repeat of the other day."

"Yes. I've never been surer about anything in my life. For as long as I'm in town."

"Let me make this clear." Dylan cupped her face then ran a hand through her hair. "There won't be any going back this time. I mean that. No time to think about it. Marcy, you think about this on the way home. This won't be another one-night stand. I want you for as long as I can have you, as often as I can."

She savored the intensity of his look and the anticipation of what was to come, confident of her emotions for the first time in years.

Dylan couldn't be sure what had changed Marcy's mind. Yet he was pleased that something had. He would have kept his word, but it had begun to take its toll on him. Since college he'd been in love with Marcy. Still, he'd been determined not to push her. She would have to come to him. With her willpower he hadn't been sure she would do so anytime soon.

More than once he'd wanted to bring the subject up but didn't dare do so for fear she'd run like a rabbit. Right now, the last thing he needed was for her to feel uncomfortable around him. Something had changed after she spoke to Ryan's mother and even more so since they'd been working to care for Steve. It was as if she'd seen her worth, found her place once more in the world.

Dylan didn't know where this was headed or how long it would last but he would take what he could get and cherish every moment. He'd taken the crumbs she would give him during their college years, but this time he intended they be on equal footing. He'd been crazy about Marcy then and he still was. He was going to enjoy the here and now and worry about tomorrow then.

He wasn't even sure what he wanted out of the relationship. Until he was, he couldn't make demands on Marcy. For now, they would make the most of what time they had.

When they entered the house, Marcy took his hand and led him to his bedroom, then his bed. He grinned. There was the old Marcy. Bold, determined and happy.

"Sit, please."

Bemused and intrigued, he did as she asked.

She stepped between his legs. Cupping his face, she kissed him deeply.

This was what he'd missed over the last few days. His entire life. For Marcy to come to him. To be the aggressor. Tell and show him what she needed.

"Just so we're clear—" she used the same tone as he had "—I want you. For as long as I can have you."

His hands went to her thighs beneath her simple dress and slid up them to cup her bottom. He tugged her closer as his mouth devoured hers. It felt wonderful, right, to hold Marcy again. Her soft sounds of acceptance and desire heated his blood and made his manhood tighten.

Dylan tried to pull her down on the bed, but she stepped out of his arms. Her fingers touched the hem of his knit shirt. Slowly, too much so for him, she removed his clothing. Next, she pulled the silk of her dress over her head. The material floated to the floor.

He forced himself not to reach for her.

Her gaze remained on him. "Is this enough to let you know that I want you? Want us."

Dylan cleared his throat. "Not yet but you're getting close."

Marcy smiled as she took a deliberate step toward him.

"Come here," he growled, snatching her

hand and pulling until she fell on the bed beside him.

Marcy giggled and it was the most beautiful thing he'd ever heard.

Her arms came around his neck. Warm, smooth skin brushed against his as she slid over him. She kissed him as she went.

Could life really be this good? Not with anyone else. Only Marcy for him.

CHAPTER NINE

MARCY MARVELED AT how wonderful life could be. She'd been staying at Dylan's house since the night of their date.

Now Dylan lay on his stomach across the bed with her on her back beside him. His arm rested over her middle. She admired his amazing body in the morning sunlight.

How quickly she could get used to this. But should she? When had she become such a wanton? Since Dylan came back into her life.

He rolled over. The sheet lay low on his hips. His fingers teased the lower curve of her breasts, sending a tingle of desire through her.

"Are you planning to sleep the day away?" His voice held a gravelly, sexy tone.

"No. We have to be at the hospital when the kids practice. The ball will be here before we know it."

"We need to make sure they have their song

together and the committee understands what we're going to do. I hate to tell you but you're going to have to say a few words as well."

She was glad to have the ball to focus on because it helped her forget she would be leaving the next day. As if by a silent agreement she and Dylan hadn't talked about the impending day, but she had no doubt he was as aware of it as she was.

Dylan groaned. "You're a hard taskmaster. Your mind is always going."

"You asked for my help."

"Remind me not to make that mistake again." He grinned.

Marcy couldn't remember her life being better. She lived in a 1950s sitcom of contentment. She woke with Dylan next to her, enjoyed her breakfast in a sunny kitchen with handsome company. Her morning meal today didn't consist of grabbing a protein bar and a cup of tea on her way out the door. Even when she and Josh were married, they hadn't eaten together often. He preferred the TV to her company. Sharing breakfast with Dylan got the day off on a positive note. She'd missed the daily routine of living with another person.

It amazed her how comfortable she'd become in Dylan's house. She'd started to think of it as her own. For once in a long time, she felt as if she belonged. She'd become so attached to her new life it would hurt to leave.

To go home to what? An empty, sterile apartment when all she did was work. How long had it been since she'd been this happy? To her surprise the afternoon at Stone Mountain popped into her head. She'd been happy then. And she'd been so happy in Dylan's arms last night.

She would cherish these times when she returned to Cincinnati.

Being with Dylan was almost too comfortable. It was calming to know he was nearby and everything about him soothed her. She'd spent far too many years tied in knots about life. With Dylan each day felt easier.

Marcy had to remind herself the land of bliss was only temporary. She couldn't trust herself to make a commitment. What if she let Dylan down? She couldn't chance that. Or open herself up to the possibility of pain again. Remaining emotionally distant was a must. The huge problem was she was failing miserably: she was falling for Dylan.

Hadn't she believed herself in love before

and her marriage failed? What made her think she could handle another relationship any better?

On Wednesday evening Dylan leaned back in his kitchen chair while Marcy was busy cooking their meal. Dylan dream of a life he'd never believed possible. He enjoyed the scene more than he should. He was headed for disappointment and heartache, but he couldn't stop the oncoming train. There was something quiet and easy, a rightness to having Marcy in his life. The clouds of loneliness that filled his sky lifted to let sunshine in when she was around.

Marcy looked every bit the woman of the house. She'd pulled her hair back, and her face was flush from activity. She moved around the work area grabbing dishes, stopping occasionally to stir what was in a pot on the stove.

Could she possibly want the same things as he? The idea sent a shot of awareness through him. He liked the idea too much, but did he dare try? He'd been rejected before. What if she rejected him again? Maybe it was better to leave well enough alone. Yet he couldn't let her leave without asking her to stay. For Marcy he would take that chance.

She placed a bowl on the table. He caught her hand as she went by him, pulling her into his lap. Wrapping her arm around his neck, she kissed him.

"Marcy, I want us to figure out some way to stay together. To explore what we've started."

She shifted off his lap and looked down at him, shaking her head. "That's not what we agreed to." She waved a hand between them. "This was only until I leave. We knew we were only borrowing time."

"Can't you feel how things have changed? How good it is between us."

"Yeah, but I live in Cincinnati, and you live here. My job is there. Yours is here. I don't see how we can make that work. I have to focus on my work. If TM13 is successful I need to build on it. I won't have time to come back and forth here. Or spend time with you if you come to Cincinnati."

"I wish you wouldn't use your work as an excuse. You hide behind it. I think we have something real, something worth building on. You can work anywhere. We have labs here."

The heat of panic washed through Marcy. She shook her head more than once, wanting him to stop talking. Dylan's face blurred from the moisture in her eyes.

He reached out to her. "Marcy…?"

She took a step back. "I'm sorry if I've led you to believe that I can give more. You deserve better than me. I'm not a good risk."

Their looks met and held. "I believe you can give me all I need and more. You have a large capacity for love. Even your work is a sign of that. You just need to believe in yourself and me."

"I won't take the chance of hurting you. I won't live through the pain of knowing I did."

"Life doesn't hold promises. Who says we can't live happily ever after? I'm confident that if we want that, we have to at least try. It may not always be good but what I can promise you is I'll always be by your side. During the good or the bad."

She frantically shook her head. "I'm sorry if I've led you to believe that I need or want more than just the last few weeks. I didn't intend to. We've been playing house and I thought you understood that. I'm not who you need for the long haul. I would just disappoint you. There's someone out there for you, but it's not me."

Dylan said quietly, "It can't be you, or won't be you?"

She paused. Her chest tightened as her ears buzzed. "We don't want the same things in life. You want a family, and I can't give you that. All the baggage I was carrying a week ago I still have. It hasn't gone away. I don't trust myself any more than I did."

Dylan stood. "So because you're afraid you won't even take a chance on us? I've seen you change over the last few weeks. I know I have. We've made a good team with patients, the ball. In bed. I think if we work together, we could make this work too.

"Your fear is going to make you throw away what might be something wonderful. What's your plan? To go through life all by yourself. Hiding in your lab. Running from anybody who cares about you or wants to get close. Spending a few weeks in bed with the next man then moving on."

Marcy flinched. The idea of being with anyone but Dylan made her sick. He made her sound pathetic. She snapped, "You're the one that pushed that. I tried to tell you. You're no better. You were rejected by your parents, your fiancée, and you keep your true feelings closed off. How do you know you don't want me just because you no longer want to be alone? That I don't just fill a missing hole in your life? You haven't even said anything about how you feel about me? For all I know you just want me for the sex."

He took a step back as if she'd slapped him. "I said I wanted us to see where this goes."

She glared at him. "That's not the same as saying you love me."

His voice had taken on a tight note. "If I said that would it made a difference?"

She shook her head.

"Then why put my heart out there for you to stomp all over it? I've had that happen enough."

"Apparently I'm not the only one with fear issues."

"I may be closed off emotionally but I'm not using my job as a gilded cage, a reason not to rejoin the world. You're keeping your head buried in a lab, staying alone, half living. You have too much love to offer, too much vitality and the desire to live to the fullest to hide it. This past week has shown me that. I've watch you blossom since you got here. You are different. A good different. It's going to come out some way, I can promise you that."

"You don't know the pain of loving and losing it," Marcy all but spat.

"I don't? I watched you walk off with another guy in college. I know what it's like to spend my Christmases and birthdays away from my family. I know what it's like to be second in people's lives. You can bet I have an idea about love and loss."

She sucked in a breath as if something had hit her. "I'm sorry, Dylan. I won't add more hurt to your life, and I would. I don't trust myself not to."

"Not even enough to take a chance on us seeing what this could be. I'm not your ex-husband. I can't bring back Toby, but I can offer you a chance to have everything you ever dreamed of. All you have to do is reach out and take it." He offered his hand, palm up.

Marcy looked at it. A tear ran down her face as she silently shook her head. One of them must be realistic.

Dylan let his hand drop to his side, his face a mask of sadness and disapproval.

Unable to say anything to make him feel better, she went to what had become their bedroom.

* * *

Dylan dropped into the chair. That certainly hadn't gone as he had hoped. He wanted Marcy to wrap her arms around his neck, kiss him and say she would give them a try.

He thought they'd gotten past her earlier anxiety. But apparently it was so deeply embedded in her she couldn't see the iron door she'd bolted between living life and existing. Only, in the last few weeks he'd seen her open the door but tonight she'd firmly slammed it in his face.

Dylan sat there until well after dark. He went to his bedroom and wasn't surprised to find it empty. Stepping down the hall he found Marcy lying on the guest bed. She was curled on her side with her back to the door. He wondered if she was asleep or pretending. Still, she looked as unapproachable as a fortress wall.

He returned to his large, cold, lonely bed. As sleep slowly found him, he continued to rack his brain for some way to get past the wall Marcy had built around her heart.

Dylan woke to the sound of movement in the house. He stepped into the hall. Looking into the guest room, he found the bed tightly made. The irony didn't escape him: just like

Marcy's feelings. In the kitchen, he noticed the door ajar.

Marcy entered. She jerked to a startled stop when she saw him. "Uh, I didn't mean to wake you. I'm sorry."

"What are you doing? Sneaking out?" Dylan glanced out the door at her car. "I see you're all packed up."

"All except my purse and I'm getting that now." She turned away slightly.

"Marcy." She finally looked at him. "Don't you think we need to talk?"

She hung her head. "I think we said everything last night."

If she'd hit him in the chest it couldn't have hurt more. He stepped aside. "Okay, then I'll get out of your way."

Neither of them said anything as she retrieved the rest of her belongings. His heart sank. She was cutting him out of her life.

"You'd rather stay in a sad little apartment than be here with me." He couldn't hide his bitterness.

"I won't be there long. I'm leaving for Cincinnati today." She headed for the back door.

"When did you decide that? The Care Ball is next Saturday. You're going to miss it. The kids will be heartbroken if you aren't there."

He couldn't believe she would just run away like this.

"I'm sorry. You'll have to tell them I had to go home," she said in a soft, sad voice.

"What about your trial?" His chest hurt as if he'd been stabbed. Once again someone he cared for was walking out on him. Was that always going to happen to him?

"I have all the numbers I need right now. The others I can call and get from one of the nurses," she called over her shoulder.

"Marcy, it doesn't have to be this way." He wanted to go after her and beg her to stay but what good would that do.

"I think it's best for both of us." She still wasn't meeting his eyes.

"I know you're running." He couldn't let her get away with this without a fight.

"I'm not going to argue about it. Dylan, this is the way I want it." The pain in her voice made him question if it really was.

"Apparently," he snapped.

She put her hands on her hips and leaned toward him. "Don't act like I'm the only one with issues hanging over my head. You don't think I'm dealing with mine and I know for a fact you're not dealing with yours. With all your talk about running, you're doing your own version too. Why haven't you made it clear to your dad you'll never be joining him? You don't owe him anything. He certainly wasn't there for you. Instead, you're letting him believe there's a chance. You aren't being fair to him or you."

Dylan took a step back as if she'd slapped him. "Wow, I didn't see that coming. Are you lashing out at me because you don't want to see it in yourself?"

Her eyes widened as if she were surprised, he'd come back at her. "I think I'd better go."

"You do what you need to do. I wouldn't want to hold you here any longer than necessary." Dylan might regret his tone of voice later but right now he was hurting.

Marcy said a civil goodbye and drove away. Dylan stood in the driveway watching the back of her car go down the street, filled with loss and defeat.

CHAPTER TEN

DYLAN WAS MISERABLE. In every sense of the word. He'd believed that his other disappointments had hurt—events when his parents couldn't attend, Beau leaving so abruptly from school or even his fiancée dumping him at the last minute—but none of that compared to what he felt at the loss of Marcy.

What really bothered him was he believed she'd been happy with him. That she had changed her mind about their time together being short-lived.

He shook his head as he drank his coffee and looked out into the gloomy sky over his back garden. Even that reflected the situation and his mood.

Over the last few days he'd spent his time going through the motions of life. Marcy was gone. He missed her so deeply there was a never-ending ache in his chest.

She'd packed up and moved out of his office before he made it to work. He wouldn't have been surprised if she'd gone in under the cover of darkness to take care of it before returning to the house to pack. There had been a note on his desk saying somebody would be in to remove what was left of her stuff. As if he cared about her desk being taken away.

Her presence lingered regardless. He couldn't find a place that he didn't associate with Marcy. The hospital reminded him of her. His office still smelled of her. His house no long felt like home without her.

Marcy not only vacated his office, but she had vacated every area of his life. It had left him floundering. He'd sworn he would never be in this position again. Rejected. He'd let her in and now he was paying for it.

Once she'd only been a memory of the girl he couldn't have from college, but in a short time she'd become his world, and then left it with a gaping hole. He had no idea how to fill it.

Why couldn't they talk this out? Marcy never once said she didn't care about him. He'd called her but got no answer or return call. It was as if there had never been anything between them.

When he'd suggested they might have a future together he'd had no idea he would get such a volatile reaction. They'd been getting along so well. He'd never been happier or looking toward the future more. Apparently, he'd completely misread her. He couldn't understand how he had misjudged her feelings so acutely.

The phone rang. He went to the kitchen and picked it up off the table.

"Hey, buddy. I was just checking in about this weekend. Lisa and I are still planning to be there for the Care Ball."

"Good. I look forward to seeing you guys." Dylan tried to put enthusiasm into his voice that he didn't feel. "You're welcome here."

"Thanks, but we're going to a hotel. We're planning a little second honeymoon since the kids won't be with us." Beau sounded pleased.

"Sounds like fun." Dylan wasn't sure anything sounded like fun to him these days. He sank into a chair.

"I understand from the committee you have a special program planned."

Dylan wanted to groan. That would be the one he and Marcy had worked so hard to put together. Every day at least one of the patients or parents planning to attend the ball asked him about her. If he wanted her out of his life it would be impossible to achieve because he had constant reminders. But he didn't want her out, so those questions made it more difficult for him to survive her loss.

"I think you'll be impressed." If people were, it would be because of Marcy's efforts. It was her idea. Her leadership. Her natural interactions with the kids and parents made it come together. And she wouldn't even be there to see it.

"I hope it's not another one of your riveting speeches again this year." Beau's tone was teasing.

"I'll have to say a few words, but I promise to keep it short." Dylan didn't even feel like attending but he had no choice. He'd put on his happy face and go do what must be done just like he always had when someone had let him down.

"Dylan? You okay, buddy?"

"Yeah. Why?"

"You sound like something's bothering you."

Concern rang clear in Beau's voice. Dylan wasn't sure he wanted to rehash his actions and feelings regarding Marcy. Still doing so might help him think through what to do.

Beau was his most trusted friend. He always gave sound advice.

"It's about a woman."

Beau hissed. "That kind of problem. What's her name?"

"Marcy."

Beau's tone turned thoughtful. "Wasn't that the name of the girl you were so crazy about in college?"

"The one and the same."

"Really?" Beau sounded intrigued. "Start at the beginning."

Dylan left nothing out as he told Beau about his and Marcy's time together. He finished with, "I don't know what to do. To make matters worse this ball is like pouring salt on a wound."

"Lisa and I wondered when a woman would come along who would make you sit up and notice longer than two dates." Beau sighed. "I'm not particularly good at the love advice but my suggestion is you figure out how you really feel. Do you love her? If you do, then tell her. She might surprise you."

"I told her I care."

"Not the same thing. I know you've closed your feelings off to most people to protect yourself but sometime you're going to have to open up. Take a chance. You can't expect her to if you aren't willing to try."

"Have I really been that bad?"

"How long did it take you to get over that rotten fiancée of yours? I hear more pain in your voice over Marcy leaving than you ever had over a wedding being canceled."

Dylan couldn't disagree with Beau.

"I suggest pouring your heart out. Trust your feelings, respect hers, and maybe she'll come around."

"I don't know about that. She's been knocked down harder than most. She's running scared. I'm not sure she'll listen to me."

Putting pressure on her wasn't what he wanted to do but the longer they stayed apart the more difficult it would be to convince her they could make a life together. He believed that without Marcy his life would always be missing that special element. They belonged together. He just needed her to see that.

"I don't know if I have a chance."

"Sounds like you're scared. You'll never know unless you put yourself out there. Something you haven't been willing to do for years. You better decide how much you want her."

"At first I wanted to give her some time

to think. Now she won't answer my phone calls."

"I suggest you pack your bags and go after her before it's too late."

"She was adamant about not wanting to talk to me." Dylan fiddled with his coffee cup, twisting it around on the table.

"That might have been the case then, but what about now? She may have changed her mind. You know I had to convince Lisa I was the guy for her. I had to keep in front of her until she realized it. Lisa and I are always in your corner. We want to see you happy. It's time for you to stop brooding and go after her. Convince her you should have a life together."

"Okay. You've persuaded me. I'll get through the ball and then go to Cincinnati."

"Sounds like a plan. We'll see you at the ball. Talk more then."

"I appreciate the pep talk."

"Anytime, buddy. You've been there for me when I've needed you. Just returning the favor."

Marcy carefully slipped the test tub into the holder on her lab table in Cincinnati. She couldn't believe she'd done it. Had let it happen. The one thing in the world she'd tried to protect Dylan from was her hurting him. He deserved better than that. But she'd failed. Again. All she'd managed to do was make them both unhappy.

She couldn't look him in the eyes as she'd left his house, and even resisted looking in the rearview mirror. Earlier that night she'd slipped out to the hospital to take care of her office, then returned to the house to get the last of her belongs. It was almost a clean escape until Dylan showed up. She gasped for breath to ease the pain in her chest at the sight of him. The tightness reminded her of seeing the sunshine when under water and not being able to break the surface to gasp air. She struggled on but got nowhere.

The thought of returning to Cincinnati should have distracted her. She had some exciting research material to share yet it held no appeal. Atlanta felt more like home than where she lived. More than once she wanted to pick up the phone and tell Dylan she'd changed her mind, but she stopped in midmovement. She couldn't trust herself to be who Dylan needed in his life. It was best this way. At least that's what she kept telling herself. Daily.

That didn't mean her heart listened or that

it wasn't broken. Not since the loss of Toby had she been this despondent.

The trial continued to go well. She would be saving children's lives with the new medicine. That should be enough in her life. When she had all the information she needed she'd write her paper and submit it to the FDA. That's what she needed to concentrate on, her work, and forget about Dylan. She'd learn to live with the loss of Dylan and her love for him. Eventually.

She'd left Atlanta under the cover of dark rain clouds. She'd gone as she had come: on her own. She had to do so before she broke down and gave in to her need to run to Dylan, to tell him how much she cared and beg him to have her. Her time in Atlanta had changed her. Meeting Dylan again had transformed her. Tipped her world. She'd been happy there, but did she deserve that?

She'd been back in Cincinnati for less than a week, but it might as well have been years. Each day dragged by. She returned to her lab the evening she landed. She should have been excited about doing so. Instead she found her work rather dull and unfulfilling. After the exhilaration of being around Dylan, her life had no spark now. She missed him and the patients, the parents.

Each evening she went home to an empty apartment where she spent her time alone not even bothering to make dinner. Quickly she learned she didn't enjoy eating by herself, and she tried cooking, but it was no fun cooking for one.

Dylan's home had felt welcoming, comfortable, as if it were embracing her. It was still difficult to face her sterile living room in her equally sterile apartment building. Her space was like a cold locker room with little personality. She missed sitting on the patio with Dylan, watching the sunset, smelling the grass after a rain and seeing the beauty of the flowers.

She tried to get back into her daily routine, but she couldn't seem to make it happen. Going through the motions was the best she could manage. She'd even started keeping regular hours which drew her coworkers' interest and comments. The only problem with having regular hours was it left her more time to remember.

Years ago, she'd promised herself she wouldn't go to this place again where depression, disappointment and despair were her only emotions. Because of her past she held people at arm's length, but Dylan had gotten beyond her defenses, under her skin and into her heart. Now she had to deal with the ongoing pain once more. She wanted it to go away.

Nothing was the same without Dylan. Her coworkers had all offered her a welcome back. She wished she could have returned the sentiment but all she could think about was what she'd left behind in Atlanta.

One evening Marcy sat slumped on her sofa with the lights off staring at nothing when the phone rang. She reached for it, hoping it would be Dylan's voice on the other end. Sadly, he stopped calling days ago.

"Hi, honey. I was just checking on you. I knew it was about time for you to come back from Atlanta."

"Hey, Mom. I returned a while ago."

Her mother sighed. "I wish you'd called to let me know. How did things go?"

"Really well. I got excellent results."

"I expected nothing less. But you don't sound excited about that." Concern filled her mother's voice.

"I am."

"But?"

Marcy had remained close to her family,

especially her mother, after the death of Toby and the demise of her marriage. Marcy feared her mother worried about her too much. "Mom, do you remember my lab partner my last year in college?"

"The one you talked about all the time. Dale, Darnell…something like that."

"Dylan." How like her mother to remember.

"That's right. Dylan. You talked about him all the time. I often wondered if Josh got jealous. What about him?"

"He's the lead doctor in the cancer clinic at Atlanta Children's."

"He is? And how is he?" Her mother sound thoughtful.

"Just as nice as ever. Funny. Very intelligent. It was nice to renew our friendship." Marcy wasn't prepared to share with her mother how much there had been between Dylan and her.

"But there was more?" That was like her mother as well. She could read between the lines.

"Yes."

"Thank goodness. I was worried you might never have anything to do with a man again."

"Have I been that bad?" Had Dylan been right about her?

"Honey, this Dylan must be a very special man to get you to even look at him. You've done nothing but work since Toby died. It was as if you died with him. Are you going to stay in touch with Dylan?"

"No. I told him it would never work."

"Oh, honey, give yourself a chance to find happiness again. Life is too short not to grasp it. It sounds like you really care for this man. There's nothing wrong or disloyal about that. It's time for you to live again."

"Mom, I can't. What if I get hurt again? What if I fail him?"

"Aren't you being a little irrational? Hurt is part of life. Happiness should be too."

Marcy shook her head. "I can't live through that kind of pain again."

"What if you don't have to? Think of all you could have." The desperation in her mother's voice surprised her. She really wanted Marcy to step out, to move on and her mother was giving her no room to slip away.

"Do you really care about this Dylan?"

"I do. But I'm so scared that I'll fail him like I did Josh," she admitted.

"You didn't fail Josh. He failed you."

Marcy had never heard her talk like that.

"I should have told you that a long time ago. Instead of being there for you, he used you as a scapegoat for his grief. He wasn't the man I believed him to be."

"Mom, I've never heard you talk like this."

"I should have before now and you might not have wasted so much of your life hiding from it. Do you think Dylan loves you?"

Marcy's voice lowered. "I think he does."

"Then don't let fear hold you back from finding happiness." The determined note in her mother's voice made Marcy sit straighter.

"He wants children. I don't know if I can do that again."

"Oh, honey, you were a wonderful mother." Compassion circled her mother's words. "You will be one again."

"My work is here. He's in Atlanta. It's just too much to deal with."

"Not if you want to be with him and he wants to be with you. You'll figure it out. The real question is, are you happy without him?"

Marcy didn't have to think about that answer. "No. I'm so miserable I can't think straight."

"Then you can only be happier with him. The way I see it is you're being offered happiness and only you can decide if you want to take it or not."

"I don't know if I can."

"Talk to him, hon. Work it out."

"It may be too late." Marcy couldn't stand the thought of that being true. "There's a ball on Saturday. We were working together on the program. I ran out on him. He may not forgive me. I've treated him badly."

"Then I suggest you go find that perfect dress, pack it and get a flight to Atlanta. Don't think about it. Just do it. If you don't, you may regret it. I'll let you go so you can get to it, and I look forward to meeting Dylan."

"Love you, Mom." Marcy ended the call.

She pushed her hair out of her face. Her mother was right. It was time for her to take her life in hand. To stop living in the past.

Her life before and after Dylan were direct opposites. She knew what it was to have fun, to experience new things, to laugh over and enjoy simple pleasures that had been lost for too long. Dylan had brought all of that back to her life. And she'd rejected it!

No longer. She'd been half living. That had to stop. This was her crossroads and she had a choice: she could either go after happiness or she could continue to live in the past. She'd had enough of wallowing in misery. Dylan offered her a brighter future, him.

Now, if she could only push the negative thinking behind her. She must be strong enough to take hold of what Dylan offered, then she would grasp it with both hands and never let it go.

She had a few more calls to make before she went after that dress. She hoped Dylan liked surprises.

Dylan tugged at his tux jacket. He preferred his T-shirt and jeans, but understood the necessity of looking the part of doctor in charge. Surveying the large ballroom of the high-end hotel, he could see the committee had done what they could to set the stage to ask for donations. From the low lighting to the tables covered in black and silver cloths and the elegance of the glassware. It encouraged a good time, which should translate to money given.

Still, he wondered why money spent getting a hotel couldn't be better used as a donation without all the other stuff. Every year he questioned it. The committee always assured him it took money to make money. He let it go even though he believed Beau's money would be put to better use as a donation. Some things he had to accept. He just hoped he didn't have to accept living without Marcy.

He was taking Beau's advice. Tomorrow he was going after Marcy. It was time to step out, bare his heart. Take a chance because she was worth it. After a week of her being gone, he had no doubt he loved her. His bag was packed, flight made. First thing in the morning he was gone.

All he had to do was get through tonight, then he would convince Marcy that she was his future.

He looked around the room. It was filling up.

Round tables circled the dance floor. Varying numbers of people were seated at them. The band turned up and started to play. Couples were entering the dance floor. At one time he'd looked forward to holding Marcy as they danced. Another time, he hoped.

Dylan checked his watch. The children would perform in an hour. Until then he was to mix and mingle to encourage donations. Which he didn't enjoy doing, but it came with his job.

A hand waving in the air beckoned him to Beau and Lisa's table. They stood as he approached. Beau gathered him in a hug and clapped him on the back. Dylan took Lisa in his arms, giving her a warm embrace.

She grinned. "I hear the mighty has fallen. You are in love."

Dylan glared at his best friend then looked back to Lisa. "I am but the question is, is she?"

"I wasn't sure I'd ever hear those words out of your mouth, Dylan Nelson," she said.

"I wasn't sure I'd ever say them."

They all took seats at the table. "So what's your plan?" Lisa looked at him with eager eyes.

"I'm leaving for Cincinnati first thing in the morning. I hope to bring her back or at least work out a schedule to see each other."

"I look forward to meeting this woman that finally got the great Dylan Nelson to open his heart."

"Have I really been that bad?"

Beau and Lisa looked at each other and smiled.

A waiter offered them a flute of champagne, and Beau raised his glass and said, "To Dylan's success."

Dylan took a drink. He sure hoped he had that. He noticed one of his patients at a nearby table. "If you'll excuse me a minute, I'm going over to speak to a patient."

He'd met with most of them before he entered the room. They seemed happy and excited. Mindy hadn't been among them. "Hey, Mindy. I'm glad you made it. How're you feeling?"

"I'm good, Dr. Nelson." She wore a formal gown that hung from her slim shoulders. Tonight her hair, which he knew was a wig, was piled on top of her head.

"Good enough for a dance? This isn't the prom, but we can pretend."

The girl beamed.

Dylan offered his hand, she took it, and he led her to the floor. They danced the rest of the song and then the next before he returned her to her parents.

"Thank you for the dance," Dylan murmured, bowing slightly.

Mindy giggled, color coming to her cheeks.

"I must go now. I have a job to do. See you later." He circled the room telling people about the cancer program, what he'd like to see done and encouraging them to donate. This was his least favorite thing to do. He'd much rather stick with plain old medicine.

He checked his watch again an saw it was

almost time for the kids to perform. The bandleader had been notified to expect them. The band was to stop playing so the kids could be heard without microphones. Dylan made his way toward Beau and Lisa's table. Halfway there a bopping sound started behind them.

Robby.

Dylan quickly found his seat near Beau.

Another kid joined in. Soon the room was thumping and bumping.

Lisa leaned across Beau. "Did you know about this?"

Dylan grinned and nodded.

Robby started in with his first line of the rap. "Cancer and chemo are not fun. I'd rather be at the beach, getting sun."

The kids kept the beat.

Another spoke. "That may be so but I hav to have a treatment. I'd like to give it up f Lent."

There were chuckles around the room. eryone had stopped what they were doin listen to the kids.

"The doctors and nurses at ACH heaven-sent. But in my parents' pocke they have put a dent."

That got even more laughs.

Some of the guest joined in the thumping by tapping the tables. Robby finished the song. All the kids looked pleased and those watching appeared astounded. There was a large round of clapping.

This time Robby started with a stomp of his foot. Two or three of the kids joined in until they were all involved. Robby did the complete rap himself. This one was about life.

Dylan looked around. Several people had tears in their eyes.

As Robby finished and everyone clapped Dylan made his way to the microphone.

"Those are just a few of the patients that come to our clinic. Aren't they a talented group? As you just heard. They do this in the clinic to make the time go faster."

Everyone clapped once more. "I'd like to introduce you to a few of them. They are brave young men and women."

Dylan clicked a button on a handheld remote and a picture of Robby appeared. A picture his parent had provided. "This is Robby Neels. He's sixteen and likes fast cars along with rapping. That's obviously true." Dylan grinned at Robby. "Oh, and Robby is from 'eachtree City."

Another picture flashes up on the screen.

"John Paul Walsh is a great student. He likes training dogs and dreams of being an astrophysicist."

An *oh* went around the room.

"He lives in Winder, Georgia," Dylan continued.

When he was finished introducing the kids, everyone clapped.

"If you want to know why you're here tonight these young men and women are the answer. It's not about me, or the oncology department, or even the hospital. It's about them and saving their lives, making their lives better.

"From me and my staff we appreciate you coming tonight. We hope you've had a good time so far. Everybody, I challenge you to give. Let's break a record." He was about to step down from the stage when a flash of cobalt blue caught his attention.

Marcy. Here. His eyes widened, and his heart raced. She was here.

She came up on the stage and walked toward him.

"What're you doing here?" he asked when she got close enough to him.

She smiled. "Didn't you ask me to the ball?"

He swallowed, then whispered, "Yeah."

"I'm supposed to be helping you with the program, aren't I?"

Dylan could do little more than nod like a bobble head doll.

"Hand me the microphone. We'll talk about it in a few minutes. Right now, I've got a few more announcements and these nice people are waiting on us."

There was a murmur around the room.

He gazed out at the crowd, his face heating. Marcy took the microphone, leaving him looking dumbfounded.

"Hello, I'm Dr. Marcy Montgomery. I'm a researcher whose been working in Dr. Nelson's department."

Dylan started to move off the stage.

"Dr. Nelson, don't go."

He stopped in his tracks.

"How many of you noticed that Dr. Nelson didn't need any notecards to introduce his patients?" Marcy raised her hand. People around the room joined her. "That's because he knows them. He goes around the clinic and gets to know each of them as a person. He takes time to play video games with them… which he isn't very good at." A couple of the kids snickered. "Remarkably he remembers everything about them. He's not your average doctor. I think he deserves a round of applause."

The room broke out in noise. The kids and parents stood.

Dylan hung his head in mortification. Heat filled his face. Thank goodness the lighting was dim.

"Now that you have completely embarrassed me," he hissed at her, "are you done?"

"Nope." Marcy gave him a smile. She turned to the room. "Please bear with me a minute more. I told you that I'm a researcher who has been here working in the oncology department."

Marcy looked glorious in the regal blue dress that skimmed her curves. Her hair was piled elegantly on top of her head, staying with the royal theme. Simple pearl earrings graced her ears. She left him breathless. He'd always thought her beautiful, but she was ravishing tonight. For the life of him, he'd swear he was dreaming.

Dylan saw her deep intake of breath.

"I'm also a mother of a child who died of cancer. His name was Toby. I'm working hard to find a cure and I promise you that every dollar you give will help to make that happen. Now, I hope you enjoy your evening."

Damn, Marcy was stunning in all her glory. She'd shared in public about Toby when she'd kept that secret for years. Why now? He was proud of her.

Knowing how difficult that had to have been for her, he stepped closer.

She looked at him with a shaky smile. "Dylan, do you have anything else you would like to say?"

He shook his head. There was a snicker or two in the crowd. The loudest he recognized as Beau's. He must look as bewildered as he sounded.

She continued, "Then I'll turn this back over to the band."

Dylan offered his hand to help her from the stage. With a bright smile, she slipped her hands into his. His heart took an extra beat at her touch.

"I'm so glad you're here," he said.

They had no more time before the kids surrounded them.

"You guys were wonderful," Marcy assured them as she gave them hugs.

Others came up to speak. All Dylan wanted

was to get Marcy to himself, but that didn't look like it was going to happen anytime soon.

The crowd had finally died away when he took her hand. "We need to find a place to talk."

She looked behind him.

Dylan turned and his hand tightened on Marcy's. He wasn't sure how many jolts to his system he could take tonight but this one might be the largest. Approaching them were his parents. "Mom. Dad."

His mother hurried ahead and wrapped her arms around him. "I'm so proud of you."

He held her in a hug.

When he let her go, his father stepped forward holding out his hand. "Son."

He slid his hand into his father's. The older man gripped it and pulled Dylan to him for a full hug.

"What're you guys doing here? You didn't tell me you were coming." Dylan still couldn't believe they were there.

"We got a special invitation to the Care Ball we couldn't turn down," his mother announced. "We were told that we should see how amazing our son is."

Dylan's forehead furrowed.

Before he could ask from whom, Marcy said softly, "Dylan, are you going to introduce me to your parents?"

He set aside his confusion long enough to make the introductions.

"It's a pleasure to meet you both," Marcy said.

His mother hugged her, then gushed to him, "Your patients were wonderful tonight. I was so impressed. I've heard nothing but praise for them, your program and your work."

"Thanks, Mom. It's the patients who are the stars. I still can't get over you being here."

"I'm proud of you, son," his father offered. "I don't think you've been bragging enough on your program and your importance here."

That wasn't something Dylan had been taught to do. He felt the same devotion to his work that his father did for his. He just needed his father to understand that. It was time to make it clear.

"Dad, I know you want me to come to work with you." He had his father's complete attention. "But this is where I belong. I have a practice in Atlanta where I'm doing great work that I love. I'm a cancer doctor, a darn good one. I belong here."

Marcy squeezed his hand. He appreciated her reassurance. She understood how difficult this conversation was for him.

"How long have you known this?" his father asked.

"A long time. I should've made that clear years ago. I should never have led you to believe I might join you. I'm sorry."

His father nodded. "Deep down I knew your heart wasn't in working with me. You put me off too many times when I've asked you about joining me."

"I didn't want to hurt you."

His father studied Dylan. "I can tell by the way you talked about your patients that this is where your heart is. I should have been paying closer attention to you. I would love to have you working with me, but I do understand your passion for the work you do. It's important too."

For once in Dylan's life he believed his father understood. Maybe there was a chance they could find some of what they'd lost. Dylan's throat tightened. "Thanks, Dad." He cleared his throat. "What I *can* do is come down a couple of times a year to fill in, help or give you time away. I believe in the work you do as well."

* * *

Marcy blinked back the moisture threatening to fall. What had just happened between Dylan and his dad filled her heart. Maybe she'd helped Dylan heal like he had her.

When she'd called them she had been taking a shot in the dark. It could have backfired. They might have said they wouldn't come, which Marcy would never have told Dylan. The outcome had been far better than she'd anticipated.

She'd certainly gotten Dylan's attention when she'd joined him on stage. For a moment she'd feared he'd gobble her up or, just as bad, drag her off the stage. The fire in his eyes made her blood run hot. It hadn't gone unnoticed by her that he'd moved in closer when she'd shared about Toby. Dylan knew the courage it had taken for her to say that out loud to people she didn't know. He could still be angry with her, but he'd stuck by her.

She had no doubt he would always be there for her. He would never blame her or run away from her in her time of need. Dylan would always be her rock in a storm. They would weather it together.

Josh wasn't a bad guy, he just hadn't been

SUSAN CARLISLE

the right guy for her. Dylan was. Always would be.

"Mom and Dad, I'm glad to see you but I need to speak to Marcy for a minute. If you'll excuse us." His parents gave him a perplexed look as he tugged on Marcy's hand, heading for the door.

She grinned as he checked a couple of doors along the hallway to find them locked. He said something ugly under his breath as they moved on. She asked, "What's the hurry?"

Dylan found one open. On a sound of relief, he brought her inside and closed it. In one swift motion, he put his back to the exit and pulled her into his arms. His lips found hers.

When he let her come up for air she teased, "What are you doing? Don't you know you need to be in the ballroom schmoozing?"

His gaze, hot with desire, held hers. "What I need is to be here kissing you."

His mouth found hers again. Marcy's arms went around his neck. She pressed into him. She'd missed this. Needed it. Him.

Between kisses he asked, "What're...you... doing here? I didn't...expect...you." He kissed along her neck.

A shiver went through her. "You invited me to the ball, didn't you?"

He murmured as his lips moved over her skin. "I always assumed you'd be my date. I've missed you."

Her hands ran over his shoulders. "I don't have so many offers for a night out at a ball that I can afford to turn one down."

He pulled back and looked at her. "You're telling me you were here just for a date?"

"No, I'm telling you I came because you need me here."

"You couldn't be more right about that. You'll be going home with me tonight, won't you?"

"Don't you think we need to talk before I agree to that?"

"We are talking." He kissed her again.

"I mean about our future." She quickly placed a kiss on his lips.

He looked at her again. "There'll be a future?"

"I hope so."

"Then we need to talk privately. My house is a good place for that. We won't be disturbed." He hesitated. "Or have you arranged for a hotel room?"

She grinned. "I was counting on you offering me the guest room."

"You may have to settle for the larger bedroom with a roommate."

"We should be getting back to the ball. You'll be missed." She stepped away and began straightening her dress.

"I do have some friends I'd like you to meet," Dylan replied. He pulled on his jacket making himself presentable.

He took her hand as they strolled back toward the ballroom.

"You're responsible for my parents being here, aren't you?"

"I might have given them a personal invitation. Maybe shared with them how special their son is. I hope you aren't mad?"

"No. More surprised."

"I just thought they should see you with your patients and how great you are at your job," she explained then watched for any anger he might have and found none.

"How did you find them?"

"I made a few phone calls. Then it was easy." She ran a hand across her hair.

"To whom, may I ask?"

"My first was to the head of the ball committee. She told me who the major donor was whose first name is Beau and lives in Birmingham."

"I should have known."

"Beau and I haven't officially met but we have spoken a number of times." She smiled.

"And he didn't even let on when I spoke to him earlier."

"You have a good friend there. One who cares about you." Dylan needed someone like that in his life.

"I do. But I don't want to talk about Beau right now. I'd like to dance with you." He opened the ballroom door.

"And I'd like that very much."

"Come on. Let me introduce you to Beau and Lisa. Then we're going to the dance floor where I can hold you."

He led her to a table where a man with dark hair and a wide smile sat beside a blonde woman wearing a gold gleaming dress, who beamed at them as if they knew a secret.

"I'd like for you to officially meet Beau and Lisa Johnson. Beau and Lisa, this is Marcy Montgomery."

The couple stood and gave her a hug. She'd had more personal interaction in the last six weeks than she'd had in ten years. Just weeks ago, she would've run from it. Now she found it comforting, invigorating.

Dylan held out a chair for her beside Lisa. She slid into it. He took the one next to hers.

"Beau, I understand that you and Marcy had already met each other. Sort of."

Marcy said, "It's a pleasure to put a face to a voice."

"I feel the same. You told him didn't you."

"Yes. Not everything but I told him most of it."

They spent half an hour with the Johnsons. Marcy hoped she'd found new friends.

Dylan stood with his hand outstretched. "Marcy would you like to dance?"

She smiled at him as her heart beat faster, and said, "I'd love to."

He put his arm around her waist and led her around the floor. "I thought I might die if I didn't get you into my arms again." Her hand moved against his back. "What did Beau mean by not telling me everything?"

"He offered to pay for your parents airline tickets and the hotel room." She met his look. "For some reason he thought it was important that they stayed here tonight."

"I'll have to pay him back."

"I wouldn't do that. I think he felt like it was a donation to a good cause." She smiled.

Giving her a squeeze, he asked, "Do you know you're amazing?"

"I don't know about that, but I'm glad you think so." Dylan made her feel special.

"You've been full of surprises tonight, Dr. Montgomery."

"I wasn't sure how you would take them."

"You were worried I wouldn't be happy to see you?" His expression showed concerned.

"I wasn't very nice to you when I left. I was counting on your parents smoothing the way."

"I'm glad I could say what I needed to face-to-face. He took it better than I expected. And your actions? We can talk about those later."

Marcy didn't like the sound of that. "I thought it was rather nice of you to offer to work with him when you had time off. I think that'll be good for both of you."

"I do too."

Dylan leaned in close to her. "How much longer do you think we're gonna need to stay?"

She looked around the room. Half of the attendees had left.

"We've got our own business to take care of," he whispered against her ear.

"We can go."

He walked her back to Beau and Lisa and looked at them. "I love you both but it's time to go. Brunch at my house at eleven if you're interested. If not, I'll be home all day."

Beau asked with a grin, "What's your hurry?"

Dylan gave him a smirk and took Marcy's arm. "We have some business to discuss."

Dylan drove home slowly, despite his desire to hurry. Instead, he made sure to stay within the speed limit; he must be as careful about handling his discussion with Marcy. Despite her actions at the ball her courage was fledgling.

He pulled into the drive and turned off the car. "Did I tell you that you look lovely this evening?"

"I believe you did but it's always nice to hear."

Dylan took her hand. "I've missed you."

"I've missed you too."

"I'm taking you being here as meaning something." He had every intention of being straightforward with her.

"It does."

"Good. Come on, then. Let's go in and

talk." He helped her out of the car and into the house.

Marcy looked around the kitchen. "I've missed this room too."

"Would you like a cup of tea?"

"Oh, no, thank you. What I would really like is to borrow one of your sweatshirts and sweatpants and sit outside."

"That can be arranged." He started toward the back of the house.

She followed, stopping in the hallway in front of his bedroom door. "I need help with my zipper."

Dylan swallowed hard. He handed the clothing to her. Slowly he lowered the zipper, appreciating the silky skin beneath. Finished he said in a raspy voice, "Marcy, you should go to the guest bedroom, or we won't get to that talk tonight."

She grinned over her shoulder and hurried out.

He was waiting on the patio with a blanket for her when she joined him. "Are you sure you'll be warm enough?"

"I believe so." She took one of the chairs and pulled her legs beneath her.

Opening the blanket, he settled it over her

shoulders then took the chair beside her. "Do you want to go first or should I?"

"I would like to go first. I'm sorry about how I acted when I left. I was horrible to you. My only defense is that I was scared."

"It's okay. I wasn't any better." Dylan took her hand.

"Let me finish before you let me off the hook. I've been afraid for so long I hardly know any other emotion. I was afraid of how you make me feel. Of what you wanted from me, of the future and the list goes on. You were right. I had stopped living, had closed myself off in a lab.

"Being with you gave me freedom. Most of which I didn't know what to do with. You made me want things I'd long ago stopped dreaming of. That was scary. But the thing is, you helped me to start living again. For that I'll forever be grateful."

Dylan squeezed her hand.

"What I really came to say is that I love you. I think in some way I have since we were in college."

He gathered her into his lap. She came willingly. As he found her lips, she curled into him.

"I feared I'd never hear that," he confessed

then kissed her tenderly. When he pulled away, he said, "I love you, Marcy. I know I have since college. I loved the girl you were and the woman you've become. I've stayed closed off because I believed if I let anyone in, they'd hurt me, leave me. You've taught me that isn't fair.

"Like tonight, you gave me a wonderful gift. You gave my parents a picture of who I am. That means the world to me. That's not the action of someone who won't be there for me forever."

Marcy kissed his neck. "So, you're going to stay at Atlanta Children's and work with cancer patients."

"That depends."

She sat up quickly. "Depends?"

Dylan gave her a direct look. "On you. I'm not going to live anywhere without you."

A shiver went down her spine. He would give up his work in Atlanta and his home for what she wanted. "You would do that for me?"

"And much more." He took her hand in his. "Don't act so surprised, Marcy. I've already told you that I love you. I haven't changed my mind. I want us to create a life together. I'm hoping, based on what you've said, that you feel the same way. If I need to move to be with you, I will."

"You would give up everything for me?"

He brought her hand to his lips, looking into her eyes. "Sweetheart, I would do anything to have you in my life. I've been so miserable without you. When you were gone it was like the sun had gone out for me."

Moisture filled her eyes. "I'm such a mess."

He stroked her cheek. "And I love everything about you."

"Dylan…" Her mouth found his and the tender touch of her lips expressed her emotions. Warmth wrapped around his heart.

Marcy cupped his face with both hands. "It's time I stopped hiding behind the past. That I take a step forward. I feel like someone who has been released into the world. I've been thinking about what you've said a couple of times, that I need to consider helping cancer parents. I have a unique perspective as a doctor and as a parent."

"You do."

"When I was making all those phone calls to your parents and such, I talked to the children's hospital. They have a program that's really working. I want to go visit. Maybe there's a place at Atlanta Children's for one of those. If there was, I'd like to lead it. What do you think?"

He hugged her. "That sounds wonderful. I think you would be perfect for the job." He hesitated. "What about your research?"

"I could always do that. Maybe oversee it. I really enjoyed doing the trial so maybe I could coordinate those."

"For a woman who has lived in a lab for years you sure are busting out."

Marcy grinned. "It's because you showed me the key."

"What's that?"

"Love."

Dylan didn't say anything for a moment. When he did his voice sounded raspy. "Sweetheart, I hope I can live up to that."

She gave him a quick kiss. "I have no doubt that you can. You're my knight in shining armor."

"Any knight can fall off his horse."

"But you won't." She stood and tugged him toward the house. "Come on, I'm getting tired. It has been a big night. The rest of our talk can wait."

"We've covered the stuff that really matters." He lifted her into his arms with longing and desire pulling at him. "Now I want to show you how much I love you."

Dylan woke next morning to a warm and sweet-smelling Marcy snuggled against him. Did he dare believe it wasn't a dream?

Her gentle hand skimmed his chest hair. "I was wondering if you'd ever wake." She kissed a spot where her fingers had teased. "I've been thinking."

"Is that so?" He said playfully, his hand appreciating the silky feel of her hip.

She moved to lie across his chest, so his gaze met hers. "I'd like to have a baby."

Dylan tensed. His eyes widened. "Marcy, you don't have to do that for me. You and I can be happy as long as we have each other."

"I want more children. You'd be the most wonderful father. With you I can be a good mother."

For a moment Dylan could hardly breathe. He hadn't expected this. He'd accepted he couldn't live without her; the children he didn't know would just have to remain that way. "You were a good mother to Toby."

"I know that now. I'm working to let go of my guilt. I can't say I won't be hypervigilant to the point of making you crazy, but I'll try not to be."

"Sweetheart, we would be in it together. The good and the bad."

"I believe and feel that." She hugged him.

His brushed his hand over her hair. "Before I can't stand it any longer and want to get started on making that baby, maybe I should ask you a question."

"Question?"

"Yep." He reached over the edge of the bed. Picking up his slacks, he fished into a pocket and pulled out a small velvet bag.

Marcy leaned back. "What's in that?"

He grinned. "Something for you. This isn't very romantic, but I can't wait." He slipped a finger in the bag and came out with a sparkling diamond ring. "I had it ready because I was coming to Cincinnati to find you today."

"You were?"

"I was. Marcy, will you marry me?"

She leaned forward, kissing him on the lips and all over his face. "Yes, yes, yes."

He chuckled. "Do you want to maybe put this on your finger, so it doesn't get lost while I'm making love to you?"

She spread the fingers of her left hand wide. He slipped the ring on her fourth finger. "I love it. It's perfect. I'll have to tell your parents thank you."

"For what?"

"For having a nice guy like you."

Dylan's lips formed a pout. "How about thanking me instead?"

"I can do that." She wrapped her arms around his neck and kissed him.

EPILOGUE

MARCY APPRECIATED THE warmth of the Sunday morning sun streaming through the bedroom glass door. She picked up the envelope off the bed and opened it. "It's from Mindy. She's loving college and has a boyfriend. I thought she might never look at another male after she danced with you."

Dylan leaned back against the pillows resting at his back. "You saw that? You were already at the ball? You never said so."

Marcy grinned. "I was there watching from a staff door."

"You're a sneaky one," he teased.

"I know you made her evening. And that little bow at the end." She shook her head. "She almost glowed."

Dylan leaned toward her. "Would you glow if I bow to you?"

She smiled. "You make me glow all the time."

One of the two babies that lay between them whimpered.

"It's almost feeding time." Marcy rested a hand on the child, hoping to put her off for a minute.

"You know when you agreed to have babies it didn't mean that we had to have them all at once."

"Hey, you wanted children, and I provided them." She couldn't help the pride in her voice.

This time he leaned over enough to give her a quick kiss. "By the way, I got a note from Robby saying he has a small music contract. Pretty nice."

"He has talent. Even two years ago I could see that. Have you seen Steve lately?"

"That's right, I forgot to tell you. He came in for a semiannual visit. He's doing great. I can't believe it. It won't be long until he age's out of the children's hospital. I've been his doctor since he was four. Watched him grow up." He fingered a small pink cheek. "Now I have my own to watch."

Marcy's chest tightened at the love she saw on her husband's face.

Liz, their girl, whined again. She was Elizabeth Margaret. Elizabeth after Dylan's mother and Margaret after Marcy's mother.

"It has been old home week for me at the clinic. Lucy Baker came in. Remember her?"

Marcy nodded. "Sure I do."

"She's in remission. TM13 saved her life, I believe."

"I'm glad. Thank goodness it was approved and is now being used widely at other hospitals."

"All because of my amazing wife." He smiled at her with pride in his eyes.

"Who will now be working from home part-time and keeping up the parents' cancer support group." Marcy wasn't sure she wasn't already tired.

"Hey, what time are Beau and Lisa supposed to be here?" Dylan rolled out of bed before picking up his daughter. He gave her a tender kiss on the forehead.

"Ten thirty."

He rested the small bundle in the crook of his arm, giving her a slow swing. "Then I guess we should get moving."

"We'll be moving a lot in a few minutes. Let's not get in a hurry yet."

Dylan sat on the bed beside her. "What's wrong?"

"Nothing. I'm just happy I guess." She patted her son, who would soon be awake. His name was Johnson Toby Nelson. They were calling him John. He was named after Beau. Dylan had asked if she would like to honor Toby by John sharing the name. She'd cried into Dylan's shoulder. What had she done to deserve such a man? This life?

"You don't sound happy?" Concern laced his words.

"I am. I'm so filled with happiness."

Dylan's eyes twinkled. "Even with moving?"

Marcy had to admit they needed a larger house, but she'd fallen in love with this one just as she'd fallen in love with Dylan. "Well, maybe not that."

"At the new house I'll plant the garden. Then when we sell it many, many years from now the person can appreciate the flowers your husband planted for you."

"That sounds nice." Still, she would miss her garden here.

John whimpered.

"I guess quiet time is over." She brought her precious baby into her arms.

"Dylan," she said, sounding distracted as she gazed at him holding their daughter. "Thank you."

"For what?" A perplexed look came over his face.

"For saving me from me. I love you."

"Honey, you're the one that saved me." He gave her a long kiss.

* * * * *